EMMA HART

NEW YORK TIMES BESTSELLING AUTHOR

Cover Design and Formatting by Emma Hart
Editing by Ellie at Gray Ink

THE DATING EXPERIMENT

CHAPTER ONE

CHLOE

Not all Mondays are made equal.
Some start with you spilling your coffee or starting your
period.
Others start with unsatisfying sexual dreams about your best
friend's brother.

.

IF I GOT ANOTHER DILDO BROCHURE ON MY DOOR, I WAS going to scream.

Sure, this was New Orleans, and there were sex shops everywhere, but I didn't need them on my door, either. Not to mention that walking into a sex shop wasn't my thing.

I much preferred the privacy of online.

There were two reasons for why I was getting these brochures. Either the mail person was so useless they couldn't tell the difference between mine and Peyton's offices, or I was being punked.

I wouldn't be surprised if Dom was behind it. It was the kind of shit he'd pull just to piss me off.

I rolled up the brochure and, barefoot, crossed my office and the hall to Peyton's. "Hey," I said, opening the door. "This came in the mail and I—"

I stopped dead at the sight of the little blonde girl on the sofa. Almost as quickly as I registered Briony's presence, I whipped the brochure behind my back, so she couldn't see it.

No matter. She was engrossed in a video on a tablet with a bright pink case. She didn't even know I was here.

"What's up?" Peyton asked, rolling her chair to the side so she could see me around her huge PC screen.

I glanced at Briony and pointed, raising an eyebrow in question.

She sighed. "Elliott had to go fix something for an old lady in Baton Rouge, so I said I'd bring her to work with me until his mom is done at the spa."

"Baton Rouge? Don't they have builders? That's a good hour and a half away."

She held out her hands. "Apparently, he did work for her before she moved from New Orleans to be closer to her daughter. She's set in her ways."

"No kidding." I glanced again at Briony. "I can't compute you looking after a child."

"I lived with Dom for twenty-two years, Chlo. I'm sure I used to babysit him, not the other way around."

There, she had a point.

"True story," I said.

"What came in the mail?" she asked. "Is it behind your back?"

"Yes, but it's not a discussion we should have around her," I said, nodding my head toward Briony.

Peyton held up a finger and slid her chair to the other side. "Hey, Bri?"

Nothing.

"Briony," she repeated a little more firmly.

She looked up and over at her. "Yeah, Peydon?"

"Sweetie, can you put your headphones on for a few minutes, please? I need to talk grown-up stuff with Chloe."

"Okay, sured." Briony picked up the cord of the headphones I hadn't noticed until now. Sticking out her tongue, she put the end into the tablet with great precision, then put the headphones on her head. After a moment of adjustment, she gave Peyton a thumb up.

Peyton responded with the same, including a cheesy smile, and slid back over toward me. "Okay, shoot."

I tossed the brochure on her desk. "Is this yours?"

She picked it up. Amusement slowly curved her lips, and when she looked up at me, her eyes sparkled. "No. Why do you have it?"

"Ugh." I dropped into the chair on the other side of her desk. "They've been getting delivered to me for the last few months. I didn't sign up for them."

She snorted, only just controlling her laughter. "Sorry, Chlo. Maybe a wrong address?"

I shook my head, taking the brochure and rolling it up. "Nope. They have my name on it, and the office address."

"Maybe you signed up for something, and it was one of those places who share addresses." She tapped a finger against her lips. "You know, like when you agree to marketing emails from one website, then all of a sudden, your inbox is like fucking eBay threw up in it."

I glanced at Briony again, but she didn't even move.

"She can't hear," Peyton said. "The volume of those headphones would be audible to a deaf person. Seriously."

I paused before I replied. In the slight moment of silence, I heard the low buzz of music from Briony's direction. "Kids. They're weird."

"You would know. You share an office with one." She grinned. "Did he lose his key yet?"

"I'm not going to answer that because I'm afraid to jinx it." I folded my arms over my chest, still holding the brochure. "It's been three weeks, and I think that might be a miracle."

Three weeks after the big blow-out fight at Peyton's house, I'd relented and given Dom his key back.

It was amazing. He could find Where's Wally in minutes, but his key? No. He couldn't find that if it was in front of his face, and if he did find it, he tormented me by hiding the damn thing in various places around the office.

Tylenol bottle. A drawer. A vase. Down the sofa.

All places I could and did find them. We'd basically existed in a state of neither of us admitting that we knew the other was bullshitting for a good few weeks now.

"He'll lose it now that you asked," I muttered as an afterthought.

She rolled her eyes. "He'd lose it anyway."

"True."

"So, did you ask him yet?"

I fiddled with the hem of my shirt. "No. How am I supposed to ask him to set me up with someone when I don't want to be set up?"

"Chloe." She leaned forward, hands on the desk, palms up. "You're done, Chlo. You've literally been in love with him for most of your life, and aside from that fight a couple of weeks ago, never even been close to telling him. Even then, you said you 'had' a crush on him."

I squirmed in my seat. "I'm not in love with him."

"Chloe! For the love of God!"

"Fine." I threw out my arms. "I'll admit it, but I need to get over him, Peyt. I just don't think having him set me up with someone is the right way to do it."

"Of course it is," she replied. "Y'all are experts are matching people. Have him match you with the best possible person, and boom. You'll get over the shithead in no time."

I stared at her flatly. "If it were that easy, don't you think I'd be over him by now?"

"No. I think you're attached to the idea that he'll eventually come around. Get real, Chlo. It's not going to happen. If it would, it would have happened by now."

"Like you and Elliott?"

"Totally different situation and you know it. Dom is not good enough for you." She sat back, arms folded across her chest. "He's never shown you any sign that he's interested in you. The best thing you can do is grow a pair to ask him to find you a date."

"Whatever," I muttered. "I have work to do. Behave yourself."

Peyton burst out laughing as I turned and walked out of her office. All I wanted to know was who was sending me dildo brochures and how I could stop it.

I didn't want her dating advice. The woman had never dated until she reconnected with Elliott. Her idea of "dating" had been having sex with one person more than three times until Dom challenged her to do it without falling in love.

Not gonna lie, I was glad he refused to take her money or Mellie and I would have owed her a tidy two-hundred-and-fifty dollars each, and I was saving for shoes.

Shoes trumped friendship responsibility. Besides, I never made her fall in love.

I slid back in behind my desk, throwing the brochure in the trash. It rattled against the sides of the wire metal can before settling, half fallen over, against the wall.

I made a "psh" sound, waved my hand at it, and turned back to my desk.

How was I supposed to match people when my own life was a hot mess? I mean, holy shit. I'd spent five years matching other people, while I'd been in love with my co-worker and brother's best friend the entire time.

I could count on one hand the number of people I'd dated. I didn't even need one hand to count who I'd slept with.

Who the hell was I to match people to date?

What was I doing?

God, Peyton was right. I needed to move on. I needed to put an end to my feelings, once and for all. Me and Dom were never going to happen. That was evident when he hadn't mentioned my slip of the tongue when I told him that having a crush on him was the biggest mistake I'd ever made.

Seriously. He'd never mentioned it. Not even eluded to it.

I had to accept it. I was twenty-seven. It was time for me to stop holding onto a girlish dream and look to the future.

Not only was it pathetic, but I could literally hear my ovaries counting down. They tick-tocked at me every damn month, reminding me with the inevitably painful waterfall of a period that made me want to slice out my uterus with several forks.

Waiting for something that would never happen was no longer an option.

But how did you get over someone you'd been in love with for years? Was dating really the answer? It wasn't as if I could just cut Dom out of my life.

Hell, I didn't even know why I was in love with the fool. He was useless and prone to losing just about everything. He was a total pain in my ass who made me ridiculously mad at least three times a week.

The heart wanted what the heart wanted.

My heart wanted a goddamn idiot.

I blew out a long breath and logged into the server for the website. We each had our specialties, and similar to Peyton, my speciality was matching strong women with guys who could handle them.

It was kind of like finding the person in your life who'd remove the spider from your bathtub.

It was serious business, and you needed to choose wisely. Pussies weren't allowed.

Except, in my business, they were. As long as they were attached to a woman.

I opened the newest email in my inbox. Sometimes, the tailor-made dating style Stupid Cupid offered was intense and exhausting, and I knew I was looking at one of those situations.

She was forty-two. Single. An attorney. She was only available at specific times, and because she was a high-flier, any prospective boyfriend had to accept that cancellations were a part of her life.

I wanted to nap just thinking about it.

Seriously. The work that would go into her was exhausting, but it'd be worth it when I nailed it.

Not if.

When.

I didn't screw up my matches. Sure, they didn't always work out, but that was after a few months when clients either grew apart or their situation changed.

That was life. The natural order of things.

I should know.

I tapped my fingers against the desk as I stared at my screen. I wanted to tell this woman no, but, how could I? She needed help. It was my job.

I had no choice.

I replied to her with an extensive survey designed to help me match her with her perfect guy. Every word felt like bullshit.

Did perfect exist?

Of course, wine and wearing no pants were right up there with perfect.

If only this were as simple as that.

But guys? Were soulmates a thing? Was there genuinely somebody out there for everybody? And if there was, how did you find them?

Was it a coincidence? Did the universe plan it all? Or were some of us destined never to find our other half?

Ugh. This was too much soul-searching before lunchtime. I needed at least another two cups of coffee and half my body weight in carbs before I tackled the mysteries of the universe.

Maybe even then it'd be questionable.

I blew out a breath and walked into the small kitchen just off the side of Dom's office. A glance at the clock told me he was late, something I wasn't surprised about, even though he lived up-freaking-stairs.

I switched on the coffee machine and leaned against the small counter. The kitchenette was only big enough for a coffee machine, a microwave oven, a sink, and a small mini-fridge, but it was perfect to keep me from killing people on a semi-regular basis.

Why had I gone into a business that required me to be nice to people?

Oh, that's right. I'd been desperate for a job and unable to get one.

Desperation makes you do stupid things. Like open a dating website with the guy you've been in love with almost your entire life.

I should have had coffee before I made that choice.

Or a therapist.

Good Lord. Why had nobody stopped me doing this? And why was I now questioning it?

Because I had to move on? Because I knew there was no chance that Dom would ever see me as anything other than his sister's best friend?

Yes. Because this was awkward.

I mean, hell. I still had the lingering frustration of a dirty dream from last night. My alarm had blared at me like a freaking siren before I'd been able to, well, finish the dream. And Dom had been the person in the dream doing all kinds of deliciously dirty things to me.

Shit, I had a problem. A big, big problem.

How could I get over him if I was dreaming about him?

How the hell was I supposed to ask him to find me a date?

And what the fuck did I do if he said yes?

CHAPTER TWO

CHLOE

There aren't enough carbs in the world to counteract the amount of bullshit.
Trust me. I've tried to eat them, and all I got was an extra five pounds on my ass.

I WAS SAVED.

Dom hadn't shown up to work yesterday—and he hadn't been home, either. On one hand, it pissed me off because I had to explain to the woman who'd shown up for a meeting with him that he was sick. On the other hand, I stole her from him.

Cha-ching.

You snooze, you lose.

As it stood, he was late today, too.

How could you be late when you lived upstairs?

Oh, that was right. You made sure you weren't home.

Seriously, it was his funeral if he didn't show up today. I knew how to kill people. I'd even do time for his death at that point. I'd long since passed any ability to be empathetic with the giant child I called my business partner.

I also needed another job. The lack of my own love life was unsurprisingly uninspiring, and if I had to watch one more romantic movie to get that inspiration, I was going to puke.

The sound of the front door opening had me looking up. Dom entered the office with a big, shit-eating smile on his face.

"Oh, look. He remembered he has a job." The veiled insult jumped off my tongue before I could stop it.

He froze, still holding the door open. "Can that wait?" he hissed. "I'm with a client."

My nostrils flared, and I gripped the edge of my desk, ready to push my chair back.

I was stopped by the arrival of a tall, beautiful woman with a smile that was either a thousand-watts or the result of too much whitening.

I knew which my pick was.

She pushed some of her voluminous brunette hair behind her ear, her smile widening as the red lipstick she wore only made her teeth look whiter. It was almost too dark for her pale complexion.

Boy. I was judgey today.

"Why don't you take a seat, Ruby?" Dom said, motioning toward his side of the partitioned room.

"Sure." The smile she offered him was entirely too flirtatious, and I barely hid a snort as she walked on heels over to where I couldn't see her. The clicking of the stiletto heels against the wood floor grated on me— mostly because she sounded uneasy on them.

"I'll be right with you," Dom said, smiling in her direction.

"Sure, honey," she said with a voice that was, like her affectionate name for him, a little too sweet.

Dom nodded, still smiling, and turned to me. His smile dropped instantly, and he closed the distance of my space, stopping on the other side of my desk.

The desk I was still gripping.

I didn't care that he knew I was pissed.

"What was that?" Dom asked in a hushed tone. "You can't—"

"Don't you dare." I finally stood up, pointing my finger at him. "You're the one who skipped out on work yesterday, missing a meeting with a new client, and then is late today."

"Keep your voice down. Ruby is a client," he said in the same, low voice. "We can talk about this later."

"A client who wasn't in your appointment book, unlike Charlotte Porter who was." I glanced at my calendar. "I'm going to get breakfast." I grabbed my purse and got up, then stalked past him. "Oh, and don't be too long, because you have an appointment in forty-five minutes," I added, right before I walked out of the door without looking at Ruby.

I let the door shut behind me, and as I stopped to take a deep breath, the echo of Dom's apology to Ruby sounded in the hallway.

"It's okay," she replied in that same, sweet tone. "It's nice that your assistant is looking out for you."

Assistant? The nerve.

"Yes, well," Dom said, skipping over it. "Let's get started, shall we?"

I was going to wring his balls through a blender.

"I won't take up all your time now. We can always rearrange," she finished on a flirtatious note.

Dom laughed.

Peyton's door swung open. "What are you doing?" she whispered.

"Pretending to get breakfast," I whispered back, cocking my thumb in the direction of my office.

She nodded in understanding and stood aside. "I have donuts."

I basically ran into her office.

"Chlo, is there a reason you don't have shoes on?" She stared at my feet.

I looked down. Shit. I'd taken my shoes off when I'd gotten to work this morning, and in my frustration, had forgotten to put them back on.

"I think Dom knows you aren't going to get breakfast." She was trying not to laugh.

"I'm getting breakfast here. I didn't say I was going out," I muttered, opening the box of donuts on the table in front of the sofa. "Therefore, I am not lying."

I snatched a glazed donut out of the box and dropped down onto the comfortable sofa. Crumbs fell onto my lap when I tore a bite off, and Peyton did her best to hide her wince.

With a grin, I chewed and picked up the crumbs one by one, dropping them back into the box.

She exhaled. "You get me."

I laughed, leaning back on the sofa. "Get you, tolerate you. All is fair in friendship."

"Well," she said, picking up a donut with pink sprinkles, "if it makes a difference, I'd help you bury my brother's body."

"That went from zero to what-the-fuck really fast, Peyt."

"I saw him bring that woman into the office," she said, donut in her mouth.

Right on cue, loud, tinkling laughter came from the direction of my office.

I wrinkled up my face.

"Chloe…" she trailed off.

"I'm mad at him because he bailed on work yesterday," I reminded her. "Not because he brought a half-price hooker into my office."

"Sounds like it."

"I need to sage that office. God knows what she brought in."

"Well, on the plus side, she brought my brother to work." Peyton smirked.

"Mmm," I said, licking my fingers. "Probably only because she thought he was in the database. Or she confused our business with yours."

Peyton held up two fingers. "Scouts honor, if she comes in here, I'll match her with a teeny peen."

I held up a hand for a high five, and she obliged. "How long do you think I have before I have to go back in there?"

"Well, given that you're not wearing shoes... Although Dom might not have noticed," Peyton mused. "At least another twenty minutes."

I sighed.

At least she had donuts.

***

I walked back into my office thirty minutes later, and Ruby was still there.

Hell, she was there. She was perched on the edge of his desk, leaning over on her hand. She twirled a lock of her dark hair around a finger, and the giggle I'd heard all too many times over the past half an hour now grated on me.

I slipped into my office unnoticed as Ruby leaned down into Dom farther. I dumped my purse and put my shoes back on my feet, then headed back to his office, where I stopped and cleared my throat.

Ruby jerked around, while Dom merely glanced over the top of his laptop.

"I'm sorry, did I interrupt?" I asked, taking on my own sweet and innocent tone. "Dom, your next appointment will be here in five minutes. I didn't want you to forget."

"Yeah, I got it, Chlo, thanks," he said stonily.

Ruby giggled, touching his shoulder. "I'm so sorry, Dom. I kept you here longer than I thought I would."

Dom, almost to his credit, shied away, pulling her hand from him. "Don't worry about it, Ruby. I'll make sure to work on you this weekend."

She stood, her smile as flirtatious as one smile could get. "Oh, I hope you do. I can't wait."

Out of sight, I rolled my eyes and walked into the kitchenette. While Peyton had a steady supply of donuts, she'd been seriously lacking on the coffee. I accepted that mixing a sugar high with a donut high wasn't necessarily the best idea but screw it.

Getting out of bed this morning had apparently been a bad idea, too.

I shut myself in the kitchenette and drowned out the sound of Ruby flirting her way out of the door with the coffee machine. I'd never really appreciated the noise of the machine before it drowned out the grating sound of her fucking laugh.

God, I was petty and jealous and possessive when I had no right to be.

He wasn't mine. He never had been. He never would be.

I pulled my coffee cup from the machine before it was fully done. The remaining spits of coffee fell into the drip container, and I added my one sugar and milk, stirring it a little too vigorously.

Coffee spat onto the sides from over the rim of my mug.

I wiped it up, then grabbed the mug and leaned against the counter in front of the sink. I cradled the hot mug, blowing on the equally hot liquid in almost a steady rhythm.

"What the hell is wrong with you today?" Dom demanded, standing in the doorway of the kitchen. "Seriously, Chloe? Are you on your period?"

I put the mug down a hell of a lot more gently than I wanted to. "I'm pissed, so I'm on my period? Jesus, Dom. Not all my anger is down to my hormones! In fact, ninety percent of it is down to you."

"Here we go again." He moved to the coffee machine.

"Are you for real? Dom, you didn't show up to work yesterday, and you purposely didn't come home. I had to take your client on because you didn't call her to cancel."

"Shit," he muttered.

"Exactly. Shit!" I kicked my foot back at the cupboard. "And the first thing you do is come in here with some random woman?"

"Client," he said. "Client."

"Right. Where did you meet her? On the corner of Jackson Square while she flogged her wares? And by wares, I don't mean her artwork."

"Chloe."

"No. Don't 'Chloe' me. I don't want to hear it, Dominic."

He turned around, lifting his arms up. His eyes were a devastatingly dark green, and they met mine with an intensity that sent a shiver down my spine.

A shiver I bit back.

"All right," he said. He pulled his cup from the coffee machine and looked at me without finishing making it. He needed milk and three sugars before it was close to anything he'd drink. "Shoot, Chlo. You're pissed. You're not on your period. Let go on me. Tell me all the things I've done wrong."

Well. I was never one to back down to a challenge.

"Where the fuck were you yesterday? You weren't working. You weren't home. You didn't answer your phone. You didn't answer emails. You avoided Facebook. You have responsibilities. I don't care if you're sick like I told your clients or if you're feeling like shit. You at least need to have the balls to tell me that you're not showing your ass the fuck up here." I folded my arms over my chest as he had the dignity to drop his gaze to the side. "Then, this morning, you show up with a half-price hooker and tell me she's a client? Are you soliciting now?"

"We met in Starbucks," he said wearily. "She started to hit on me, then when she asked what I did, got all interested."

"Of course she was interested in the fact you run a dating website. Except all she wants to date is what's inside your pants."

He quirked a brow. "You know that, do you?"

"Do I look like a woman?"

Dom's eyes ran over my body, lingering on both my chest and my hips a little too long for it to be accidental.

"Knock it off!" I turned, grabbing my mug. "You're an idiot!"

"You asked!" he yelled as I walked past him. "And the answer is yes!"

"Goddamn it!" I shouted back, storming through his office and into mine.

Not that it did any good. He followed me. He followed me right through his office until he'd joined me in mine. "I'm sorry. You're right. I know she wants that, but she wouldn't leave me alone."

"Now you just sound egotistical and self-absorbed," I said.

"Look, she either wants me, or she doesn't. That doesn't change from your opinion to mine."

"Actually, it does. That's the definition of an opinion."

"You're starting to piss me off, Chlo."

I tilted my head to the side. "Oh, are you on your period, too? I hear the male period is so much worse than the female one."

Dom stared at me. "Why haven't I killed you yet?"

"Same reason I haven't killed you. We haven't got life insurance on each other."

He went to say something, then stopped. "You're right. And even then, you wouldn't be worth it."

"That's all right," I said, leaning back. "I'll kill you on my period. PMS has been successfully used for insanity pleas in the past. Win-win."

"Thank God we use security cameras in here."

"Awesome. They'll see just how much you provoked me."

"Fuck me, you're like a shark with blood, aren't you?" Dom folded his arms over his broad chest. "One fucking sniff and you turn into a savage."

"I guess your bullshit is to me what blood is to a shark. And by bullshit, I mean every time you speak. The bonus is that I can smell it miles off."

His eyes pierced mine. Strong. Sturdy. Intense. That was his gaze, pinning me in place despite the fact there were a good ten feet between us.

"I genuinely don't know how I haven't killed you yet," he said in a low voice. "But fuck me, I know why you're single."

No. You don't. You have no idea.

"Enlighten me, then." I folded my arms over my chest and held the eye contact.

His eyebrows shot up as if he wasn't expecting me to say it, but it didn't last long. "Enlighten you? You're prickly. You're snappy and short-tempered. You're incorrigibly frustrating, and you have the demeanor of a desert full of cactuses."

"Cacti," I corrected him. "And that's a repeat of prickly."

He jabbed his finger at me. "You're picky and can't help but point things out to people when they get it wrong."

"It's called education. You should try it sometime."

"I have a degree."

"Yeah, but a masters in assholery doesn't count."

"I might have a degree in assholery, but you're teaching the damn class."

"And everything I'm teaching I learned from the textbook you've written over the last twenty-five years."

Dom choked in something that sounded a little too much like a laugh, but he brushed it off before I could take even a second to revel in that. "This is why you're single. Seriously. You're so... so..."

I raised my eyebrows. "Quick-witted that mere mortals can't keep up with me?"

"Full of shit," he finished. "You're so full of shit. Nobody, absolutely nobody, could ever hope to keep up with your ability to flip between sweet and innocent angel and intolerably angry devil."

"Nobody? I doubt that. There's probably someone out there who won't piss me off nearly as much as you do." I picked up my coffee and sipped.

"I doubt he lives on this planet. Maybe not even in this galaxy."

"The same could be said for the woman who could take your shit. You lose everything, you're careless, and you're so insensitive to everybody around you. You'd need a fucking saint to put up with you."

"You need more than a saint, Chloe. You need a damn god."

"So find him."

CHAPTER THREE

CHLOE

There was a reason they called it verbal diarrhea.
It was shit.

"WHAT?" DOM FROZE AND STARED AT ME. "FIND him? You want me to search the universe for the guy who can put up with you?"

No.

Why did I say that?

I mean, yes.

I did. I wanted him to find me someone to date, but not like this. I wanted it to be a gentle conversation—like those ever happened—and not in the middle of one of our screaming matches.

But, hell. Screw it. I'd said it. I had to follow through with it.

"Yes," I replied, setting my mug down and pretending I'd totally meant to say it. "You think you can't, so find him. I bet there's someone in our database who'd be a good fit for me."

"I think you've lost your mind, Chloe."

"I dare you." My lips twitched up into a smirk. "I dare you to find me someone to date."

His jaw clenched, and the twitch at the corner of his eye gave away his frustration.

Dom was many things, but a chicken was not one of them. As evidenced by the dare he'd had with his sister about falling in love with a hook-up.

I knew he'd accept. There was no way he wouldn't. He might hate it, but he'd do it.

"Fine." He scratched the back of his neck, averting his eyes for a brief second. They landed back on me with a hard gaze that was indescribable. Stormy and intense. Dark and reserved, they made a shiver run down my spine. "But, if I'm matching you, you're finding me a date, too."

Wait.

No.

I didn't sign up for that.

"Um.... You want me to match you?" I asked warily. "Aren't you worried I'll put you with a demon of a woman?"

Dom's nostrils flared. "Yes. Terrified, actually, but it seems fair. If I'm matching you, you match me. And we both have to stick out three dates."

"What is your obsession with the number three?"

"It's the average number of orgasms I give a woman during sex," he said without batting an eyelid. "It's the magic number. It's enough to know if you're compatible with the person you're dating, but not so much you want to stab yourself with a fork."

Well. He had a point, as much as I hated to admit it.

"Fine," I replied, using the same tone he had. "I'll find you a date. But, and we both promise on this, we won't fuck around. We'll actually find each other someone decent. Compatible. Good people."

He nodded quickly. "Done. How long do we have?"

"Three is the magic number, according to you, so three days." I swallowed. "We blind date at the same time on the same day and report back the next morning."

Something flashed across his features for a moment, but whatever it was disappeared quickly, and he schooled his expression into one of indifference. "Three days including today?"

"Yes. And the first date should be Friday night." I felt sick. "Done?"

"Done," he said, voice firmer than I'd ever heard it. "What if we get it wrong?"

"Eternal bragging rights for me when I nail your date," I shot back.

He flipped me the middle finger, and without another word, disappeared.

I let go of a deep breath and sagged into my chair. Had I really just done that?

Had I really just not only asked Dom to set me up with someone but agreed to set him up with another woman?

Shit.

***

"Well, that's a hot mess if there ever was one," Mellie said, her wine glass hovering in front of her mouth.

"You are the authority on hot messes," Peyton pointed out, poking a breadstick in her direction.

The theme for tonight's girls' night had been chips and dips, so naturally, I'd loaded up on ten different dips and a variation of chips and stuff you could dip.

I also had pizza, because you could totally dip that into ketchup, so it counted.

"I want to argue, but yeah, no." Mellie shrugged. "Chlo, what are you gonna do?"

"What do you mean?" I asked around a mouthful of chips and guac. I swallowed. "I'm gonna match him. How else am I gonna get over his stupid ass? He's gonna match me to someone I'm compatible with, and I'm gonna do the same for him."

"This sounds like a disaster waiting to happen." Peyton clicked her tongue. "Trust me. I was the disaster a few weeks ago."

"But you had history with Elliott," I pointed out.

"And you don't with my brother?" She leaned forward and picked up her glass from the coffee table. "You've been in love with him since before you knew what love was, Chlo. That's history. How are you going to do this?"

"Easily." I put my glass on the table and resisted the allure of another chip dipped in guac.

I'd had a lot of time—several hours—to think about this, and I knew for a fact I had this all figured out. From beginning to end. I'd nailed it. The plan was foolproof.

Given that Dom was a fool, that didn't mean a lot, but I wasn't one. A fool, that was.

"I need to get over him. I might have strong feelings for him," I admitted. "But I'm not beyond help. Besides, I don't even like him. I think he's an intolerable human being who will, one day, be the victim on one of those Investigation Discovery murder shows."

Mellie snorted. "We're with you there."

"Pretty much," Peyton agreed.

"See? So, I figure, if I do this, it kills two birds with one stone. I meet someone who could potentially allow me to get over him, and I get to see him with someone else. It'll remind me that he's not The One." I chewed the skin on the side of my thumb. "He's The One, but not for me. I think that's what I need. To see him with someone who's compatible with him, because I'm not it."

A look passed between Peyton and Mellie.

I chose to ignore it. I didn't care what they thought—Peyton was on my ass to get over Dom, and there was no way I was wrong. Anyone who fought the way we did were polar opposites to the point that there would never be a common ground.

I knew that. I accepted that.

I was okay with that.

After all, I'd had enough time to accept that Dom and I would never be a thing. It didn't matter if I'd spent years denying how I felt about him. Some things needed to be denied.

"Seriously," I said after a moment of silence. "I'm determined to do this. I'm committed, you guys. I'm going to use this stupid challenge to get over him once and for all. It won't be hard to find a guy better than he is."

"He's not that bad," Peyton said reluctantly. "He's enough of a tool to fill an entire box, but he's not bad."

"That doesn't help, Peyt," Mellie said, tipping her empty glass toward her. "We're supposed to tell her how bad he is."

"He's my brother. I tell him how much of a dick he is to his face. She already knows that." Peyt grinned.

She wasn't wrong.

"I can't think of him like that," I said. "I need to think of him the way I do right now."

"The sexy, hot-as-fuck brother of your best friend?" Mellie asked.

"No," I said. "The huge ass pain-in-my-butt, ignorant and dickish brother of my best friend."

"How in the hell are you in love with him?"

"I don't know." That was the damn truth. I didn't know. I never had known. I just was. "But I don't want to be anymore. It's time that Chloe Collins broke free of the crap spell Dominic Austin wove on her. Sabrina the Teenage Witch wouldn't tolerate it."

"She'd tolerate it," Mellie said.

"Salem would be the opposition," Peyton added.

"Whatever." I flicked my hand in dismissal. "The point still stands. There's a freaky spell on me, and I want it gone."

"You should try self-control."

"You should try not being a bitch," I muttered.

Peyton grinned. "I have to curb those tendencies around Briony. It's a true exercise in my own self-control. You're now the outlet."

Mellie raised her eyebrows. "Make Dom the outlet."

"He's the primary one."

"Well, I'd hate to hear the shit he gets."

"I'd like to hear it," I input. "God knows he probably deserves it."

Mellie paused, a chip halfway to her mouth. "True. Hey, can I send you Jake's way?"

Peyton's head jerked around so fast I thought it might snap off her neck and spin away. "What did he do?"

Like a dog with a bone...

"He made me fire Harley today." She twisted her lips to the side that was neither a grimace or a smile.

"She was shit," Peyton said bluntly. "I agree with him. She had too many chances."

"Wow. One speech about how much of a strong woman you are, and you suddenly like the guy." I snorted. "Does Elliott know you're this easy?"

"I slept with him on the first date. Of course, he knows I'm easy."

"You were supposed to sleep with him on the first date."

Mellie sighed. "Are you sure you two weren't born siblings?"

"She'd be dead if we were," I said with a grin. "Besides, that would make my situation completely awkward, wouldn't it?"

Mellie paused, then nodded. Peyton also nodded.

"What are you going to do, Chlo? Seriously. It's not a joke. You just agreed to set him up with someone else," Mellie said softly.

I stood up and turned my back to them, folding my arms over my chest. "I'm going to set him up with someone. And she's going to be as insufferable as he is. She'll be perfect for him. She'll be super organized and patient and able to handle all his bullshit. I'll set him up with someone so incredibly meant for him that not even I'll be able to look at them and feel like he's with the wrong person." I turned, taking a deep breath. "And then I'll be able to get over him. Right? That's how it works. He'll be happy with whoever I match him with, and I can move on."

"Chlo..." Peyton pushed off the sofa and walked to me. She gripped both my shoulders. "That's not how it works. You've denied being in love with him for years, but we knew. I don't get it. I don't pretend to understand how you can possibly be in love with him, but—"

"I get it," Mellie said softly from the sofa.

We both looked at her.

She shrugged one shoulder. "Best friends are honest with each other. We haven't made our friendships last this long by bullshitting our way through it."

"I bullshitted," I offered.

"All right, so not all of us made this friendship last this long by bullshitting." Her lips twitched. "But, I get it. Dom is many things, but he's also the guy who stood up for all three of us when we got bullied in school. He shut down rumors and made sure to put the fear of God in every guy who wanted to date us."

"Didn't work with Elliott, clearly," Peyton muttered.

"Not his fault, idiot," Mellie shot back. "And you know it. Stop playing the victim."

I laughed and hugged Peyton. "She can't help it. I still don't know how she never ended up in Hollywood."

She shoved me off with a playful grin. "Mellie was saying?"

Mellie rolled her eyes. "I was saying I get it. I might even have had a crush on him when I was a teenager, but I had a period longer than it. That said, he's always had a softer spot for Chloe, so..."

"A softer spot for me?" I snorted. "We fight more than him and Peyton!"

"All right, so he used to," Mellie acquiesced. "Now, you're like chalk and cheese. Whatever. I'm just saying that I understand how you could fall in love with him."

"Fair enough."

"But I don't know if this is how you get over him," she continued, finally standing and coming over to me. "You're forcing yourself to. You're focusing on the fact you're setting him up with someone and not the fact he's setting you up on a date, too."

"She's right," Peyton admitted gently. "Stop focusing on him, Chlo. Focus on who he's gonna set you up with."

I swallowed, briefly looking down. I knew they were right. I was thinking of it all wrong, but after twenty years of being in love with Dom, I knew one thing.

Fools in love were fucking idiots.

"Okay, fine. I will," I said, wrapping my arms around my waist. "I'll focus on the guy he'll set me up with and the guy I should fall in love with."

"That's the spirit," Peyton said. "And, hey, if you can't use him to get over my brother with, you can just get under him anyway."

We all burst out laughing.

I guess, if there was a logic I had to take, it'd be that one.

CHAPTER FOUR

DOM

Fall in love, they said. It'll be great, they said.
Start a dating website with your sister's best friend.
Nobody said that. I stupidly thought it was a good idea.
Plot twist: I fucked up.

HOW THE FUCK DID I MATCH HER WITH SOMEONE PERFECT for her?

My fist fell down on my desk at the same time I clicked off yet another profile.

I felt as though I'd seen everyone that Stupid Cupid had to offer. Like I'd gone through every match and then some. None of them seemed to be good enough for her.

Shit. I was the authority on not being good enough for her.

Either that or I subconsciously didn't want to do this. Hell, it wasn't even subconscious. It didn't matter that I'd told my sister I was going to ask Chloe to set me up with someone—I never dreamed she'd actually fucking suggest it.

I dropped my head forward and buried my fingers in my hair. Fuck. The woman riled me like no other, but that was only because I couldn't have her.

I wanted her, but I couldn't have her. She tolerated me on the best days.

Was that because she'd once crushed on me and I hadn't known?

When had she crushed on me? Was she thirteen or twenty-three? How could Peyton not have told me when she knew I'd been harboring feelings for that little blonde pain in my ass?

Sisters. Women. They'd kill me one day, of that I was sure. Especially when they coordinated their attacks.

I blew out a long breath and leaned right back in my chair. Fighting with Chloe was a weird kind of pleasure—almost an addiction I couldn't break. There was something ridiculously hot about the way her cheeks flushed and her eyes lit up with emotion.

There was a fire in her. A wildfire. The kind of wildfire that would take forever and a day to put out.

And I wanted to stoke it.

But, I couldn't. I had no business stoking her, which is why I clicked on the profile of a pretty decent guy I'd be happy to match with anybody except Chloe.

He was really that—a decent guy. He had a good, steady job as a data analyzer for a national company. He was into sports, but only football and baseball—something I knew she had a soft spot for because of the tight pants—and chilled out by watching real-life crime mysteries on the ID channels. He listed Joe Kenda as a favorite, and I knew Chloe had, at one point, her entire DVR filled with Kenda episodes that she binged on.

Aside from that, he worked nine-to-five, Monday thru Friday. He was close to his family who lived in Baton Rouge, but not so close he saw them every day. He was thirty, so in her desired age-range, and owned both his house and his car outright thanks to his high-flying career.

Yeah. No doubt about it. He was the kind of stable, dependable person she needed. Someone who was as equally organized as she was. Someone who was as put together as Chloe was on a regular basis.

Because that was Chloe.

Where Mellie was a clumsy, hot mess and Peyton was a bluntly-spoken clean-freak, Chloe was the strong, dependable, steady figure in their friendship of three.

She needed someone to be to her what she was to them.

She needed that. She needed someone just as strong as she was. She needed this Warren guy.

She didn't need someone like me. I couldn't remember a thing to save my life. Losing things was my modus operandi at this point. I was almost thirty and lost my key almost on a weekly basis. I couldn't remember an internet password to save my goddamn life, and as for the milk in my apartment?

I threw it out this morning. I take my coffee black, so let's say I'd forgotten it was either in my fridge.

I was the fucking male Mellie, except forgetful in place of clumsy.

There was a reason my thirtieth birthday was this year and I was completely single. My feelings for Chloe tossed aside—I hated to admit it, but I almost needed a lesson from my fucking sister on how to keep my shit together.

Setting Chloe up with another guy was the first step to that. Getting over that blonde wildcat I worked with and had obsessed over for years was the only way I'd even begin to get my shit together.

I needed to see her with someone else. I needed to see her *happy* with someone.

I didn't want to, but I needed to.

I cracked my neck by rocking my head side to side and copied his email from his application. Bile rose in my throat as I hit the "New Message" button on the email server and pasted his email into the "To" box.

To: Warren Jones w.jones@gmail.com
From: Dominic Austin dom@stupidcupid.net
Subject: Date

Hi, Warren,

Dom from Stupid Cupid here. Are you still interested in being matched by our service? I noticed your profile hasn't been active lately, but I think I have you a potential match.

Hope to hear from you soon,
Dom

I hit "Send" before I could change my damn mind about it. The worst part about this was now having to create Chloe a profile. That was the one thing we hadn't spoken about, and since we'd only discussed this yesterday, I didn't want to message her yet for it.

How the fuck would a woman fill in a dating profile? How did they fill in ours? I wasn't ashamed to admit I typically dealt with the guys. I matched them to the girls without thinking about how they filled out their applications.

I opened one of the forms. How did I fill this out for her? Did I? Or did I sell her in the way only I knew how?

And I didn't mean the prickly, antagonistic, infuriating woman I came across on a daily basis.

I meant the woman I knew that she hated being shared with anyone.

There was only one person who could help me with this. I picked up my phone and hit the name in my contacts.

Me: I need your help.

There was no response, so I opened an application form and started to fill it in.

Name: Chloe Collins
Age: 25-30
Star sign: Pisces
Profession:

Shit.

Profession: Matchmaker
Location: New Orleans
Favorite sports: Baseball

Elliott's text came through before I could go any further.

Elliott: finally setting C up?
Me: Not by choice.
Elliott: Help coming.

I let go of a heavy sigh. Thank God. He hadn't always been my favorite person, but since he'd both broken and fixed my sister's heart thanks to her stubborn nature, I was ready for the help from anyone.

"What did you do now?" Peyton shoved open my office door and stared at me.

"The fuck are you doing here?"

"Elliott said you needed help. Here is your help." She gestured extravagantly to herself before she shut the door behind her. "And I know it's about Chloe and her date, so cut to the chase."

Girl-talk. Of course, she already knew.

"I need to fill out her application," I told her. "But I'm stuck."

Peyton rolled her eyes. "And you can't ask her to do it?"

I stared at her flatly.

"Right, no, of course," she drawled, a tiny hint of her New Orleans drawl twanging at every word. "Why would you ask the woman you're in love with to fill out her own dating record?"

"Can you shut the fuck up and help me?" I threw my hands out to the sides. "I found her a match. Help me out here, Peyt."

My sister stilled. "You found her a match?"

"Of course I did. I said I would, so I did."

"Wow. You're actually going through with it. Kudos, bro." She rounded my desk and perched on the arm of my chair.

I glanced at her. "Can you put your chest away?"

She tugged at the neckline of her shirt and pulled it right up. "Put away. Let me see what you've written so far." She snatched the mouse out of my hand and scrolled. "Jesus, Dom," she said after a minute. "This is basic. This won't get her laid."

I didn't want to get her laid. I wanted to get her a good date, not a fucking orgasm.

"Whatever. Can you make her attractive to a random stranger?"

"You can't?" Peyton quirked an eyebrow and looked at me. "You've been attracted to her for at least ten years. Surely you can do better than this."

"Peyton. I want your help, not your bullshit."

"Good luck with that," she muttered. "All right, move your ass. Let me do this for you."

"Don't make her sound too attractive." My voice was no louder than hers had been as I stood and made way for her to take my seat.

She snorted, deleting everything I'd written except the first couple of questions. "I'm gonna make her so attractive that she has every eligible bachelor in New Orleans clamoring for her attention."

I shot her a look so dark I felt my blood turn black.

"Relax, Dominic. You're getting over her, remember?" She answered my dark look with one as equally annoyed. "This helps you get over her. That's what you told me."

I perched on the edge of the desk and crossed my arms. "Fucking whatever. I don't have to like this."

"You're right. You don't." She typed. "But you do have to do it."

"Whatever. Like I said. Whatever."

"You're like a petulant teenager who's just been told to do his own laundry."

"Peyton…"

She sighed and turned in the chair. "Dominic, if you're not going to admit to her how you feel about her, then shut the fuck up and suck it up. You don't get to whine about something you're unwilling to act upon. You have the potential to change the situation you're in, but you won't. It's that simple. End of."

"It doesn't matter what I do or don't say to her. She hates me. Every time we speak, we fight. She. Hates. Me."

"Yeah, well, I hated Elliott," she said, turning back to the computer. "Now I paint his daughter's nails, bring her to work, braid her hair, cook her dinner, and read her bedtime stories."

"Congratulations, Saint Peyton."

"Don't go that far. I accidentally taught her how to say 'fuck.'"

"How do you accidentally teach a three-year-old to say fuck?"

She shrugged and glanced at me. "Apparently, she was saying fork. Toddlers. They can't pronounce shit for shit. Totally not my fault. Nobody wrote that in the handbook for girlfriends of single dads."

"That's a handbook?"

"No, but I sure as hell wish it were." She shook her head turned back to the screen. "I'm winging it more than a flock of migrating birds, but whatever."

"Does that mean I'll be known as Uncle Dom soon?" I smirked.

"Nobody needs you as their uncle, Dom. Unless you count losing things as a life skill."

"I still have the photos of you grinning while making your Barbies have sex."

She waved one hand, expertly typing with the other. "Puh-lease. Literally every woman who ever owned Barbies made them bone Ken. And you know what happened? The awkward toddler called Sally. Wait, no. Sophie? Shelly? Whatever it was. Unless you had the pregnant Barbie, then your newborn went from breastfed to tantrum quicker than a Ferrari can get from zero to sixty."

I coughed. "I can't help but feel this conversation has taken a weird turn."

"It's following after my life." She peered over at me with a grin.

She could claim that, but she was happier than ever. And I was happy for her. Despite how much we bickered, she was still my baby sister. Seeing her happy was all I'd ever wanted. I'd take a bullet for her if it came down to it.

Shit, I'd take an army for her.

"No shit," I said. "Can we get to the point now?" I gestured to the computer screen and Chloe's profile.

"Right. Sorry." Peyton turned back to the screen. "Well, don't crowd me. I can't make her attractive if you're peering over my shoulder and judging me."

I made a non-committal grunting sound and headed for the kitchen.

She was right.

I was totally fucking judging her.

***

"Here." Chloe dropped a paper-clipped collection of sheets onto my desk. "Your date for your approval."

I looked from the Post-it note labeled sheets to her—to how her blonde hair curled over her shoulders and over her breasts. To the hard, downturned set of her lips and the coldness her gaze hinted at. "Approval? We're doing approval?"

"Not officially, but I wanted to make sure she fit into your ideal." She folded her arms over her chest, cocking a hip to one side. "So I thought I'd share her with you."

Was she blonde with blue eyes and red lips and so sassy my cock twitched at the mention of her name?

I doubted it.

I picked up the sheets of paper and held them out for her. "You're good, Chlo. I don't need to see it. Unless you require approval of who I chose for you," I added.

She snatched the sheets back. "Can I say I don't trust you?"

"If you want to state the obvious, sure."

Her lips formed a pout before she smacked them together. "I'll take the risk. Make sure your Friday is free. She" —she waved the sheets— "is free then. I'll let you know further details."

"Perfect. From what I know, your date is free Friday, too." I leaned back, clicking my pen against my desk as if I didn't care.

I did.

I also knew that pens clicking—themselves or against desks or otherwise—ground on her. Clicking pens were to Chloe what people who ate with their mouth open were to regular people.

"Fine." She put her hands on her hips, jerking her head so her blonde curls flicked over her shoulders. "Then we can report back on Monday."

"That's a lot of time to get laid." The words escaped me before I could stop them.

"Sure it is," she drawled. "If you have the stamina of a water pistol."

"You need Nerf water pistols."

"No, I need a battery-operated Nerf."

"But that won't cook you breakfast."

"I can cook my own breakfast."

"So can Gordon Ramsay, but I bet he still pays people." I raised my eyebrows. "Point is, we both have a date on Friday night. We can have breakfast on

Monday to reconvene and see where we go next, just like we do with our clients. Deal?"

Chloe's lips twitched, but not upward. They just... twitched. "Deal."

CHAPTER FIVE

CHLOE

Dates are awesome.
Your birthday. Christmas. Halloween. Fourth of July.
With an actual person?
Not my favorite.

WARREN JONES WAS PERFECT.

Scarily so.

We shared a table at Billie's restaurant. It was a small table, in the corner, barely close to the window. We had the slightest view of Bourbon Street, but it didn't matter because I'd chosen the right seat.

Three tables across from us were Dom and his date. Rachael Amoret. She was blonde and tanned and beautiful. She was a marketing consultant with the fullest lips and darkest brown eyes and the opinion that only a business owner could handle her obsessive lifestyle.

My back was to them, though. All I saw was the sleek, dark hair of Warren Jones. His enviable dark eyes. His square jaw that was so clean shaven he could be used in razor advertisements.

I was so fucking glad I couldn't see Dom. It was bad enough I could hear her. She had the kind of laugh that could rub against a cheese grater and make a rock cry.

And she laughed. A lot. God knows why. Dom wasn't *that* funny.

"So, you co-own the dating site?" Warren said, taking a sip of his beer after.

I nodded. "Straight down the middle. Fifty-fifty."

"How did that come about?" He looked genuinely interested, pushing his finished plate aside and leaning forward. The light glinted off his eyes, making the greeny-gray hue of them shine a little brighter.

"Well, I've known Dom my entire life. He's my best friend's brother—she actually runs our sister hook-up site."

He half-choked on his beer. "Pick-A-Dick?"

I quirked a brow, barely able to hide my smile. "Familiar with it, are you?"

His eyes widened. "Not me—I mean, yes, but I haven't used it personally. A friend signed up. That's actually how I found Stupid Cupid. Your sites are linked, aren't they?"

Nodding slowly, I cupped my wine glass. "Sometimes, we get people that come to us who don't want anything serious, and sometimes Peyton gets people who want something serious. It's easy to refer since we share the same office building."

"That makes perfect sense. So, you started this with her brother?"

"Yep. Well, actually we're all in business together, but since it's split, Peyton holds half because she runs Pick-A-Dick alone." I paused. "But we technically see more people because there are two of us. As for how it started... I was kind of lost, and when Peyton got the idea for her site, Dom brought up the idea of a sister dating site, but he couldn't do it alone. I happened to be there when the conversation happened, and that's that."

"Fascinating. Do you work well together?"

"We work together incredibly well, but we don't exactly get along."

His eyes twinkled. "Yet, he set you up."

"We kind of made a pact," I said slowly, twirling my glass. "We both set each other up."

"Were you worried he would screw you?"

"A little," I admitted. "I wouldn't put it past him."

Warren raised an eyebrow. "Did he screw you?"

I blushed lightly, briefly dropping my gaze.

No, he hadn't. Warren was handsome and polite. He was beyond attractive, and we had a lot in common from the conversations we'd had so far. Dom hadn't screwed me; he'd actually done well.

And I wasn't entirely sure how I felt about that.

"No," I said with a slow smile, still fiddling with my glass. "He didn't."

A grin broke across his face. "That's what I was hoping to hear."

Another blush tickled at my cheeks.

What did I say to that?

Why was I so

awkward?

"That's, um, good?" I said, half asking him.

His grin didn't waver. "So, I guess the question is: are we having a second date?"

"Do you want a second date?" I couldn't help my own smile as it tugged my lips up.

"I would love a second date."

"I think I can fit you in," I teased, tucking my hair behind my ear.

Warren's eyes sparkled. "Perfect." He checked his watch. "I actually have to put an end to tonight—I have a red-eye flight tomorrow for work. Do you mind?"

I checked my own watch for the time. It was nine-thirty—not exactly early for a dinner date. "Not at all. I have an early appointment tomorrow myself."

We shared a smile, and he signaled for the check. It was brought straight over, and he picked it up before I could even steal a glance at it.

"How much?" I asked, reaching for my purse to get my wallet.

"I've got it," he said, opening his own wallet and pulling out some cash.

"At least let me cover the tip."

He shook his head. "Absolutely not. I couldn't sleep tonight if I knew I'd let you pay for anything."

"Okay, but the second date is on me. And no, that's not up for discussion."

He put the money on the little silver tray with a half-smirk in my direction. "That's fair. Do you mind if I use the bathroom before we leave?"

"Not at all. I'll wait." I smiled.

He slid his chair back and used the table as leverage to stand, revealing his tall, firmly-built frame. His broad shoulders blocked out the light of the hanging bulb behind him for the brief second until he moved.

My eyes flitted to his back as he left. His light-blue shirt hugged his upper body to perfection, and it was tucked into navy pants, ones that hugged a peachy ass and were perfectly pressed down to his ankles. Shiny, dark brown shoes looked as if they squeaked against the polished, hardwood floors.

I stared until he disappeared. I caught Dom's eyes as I looked away from the restroom door, and he raised one eyebrow.

My cheeks burned.

Why the hell was I blushing? I didn't need a reason to be checking Warren out. The guy was incredibly good looking and had a body that looked as though it was worth every inch of my ogling.

Plus, he'd known what he looked like when he set us up. He had to know he was ogle-worthy.

My phone buzzed in my purse. I extracted it from the depths of my Coach purse and unlocked it. A text from Dom was flashing on the screen, and with a frown, I opened it.

Dom: Are you on a date or casting for a porn movie?

That was a bit freaking rich.

Me: Why don't you focus on your own date instead of what I'm doing on mine?

He actually looked up from his table and glared at me. I shrugged a shoulder and, with a quirk of my eyebrow, shot him a, "So, what?" look, complete with a stony curl of my lips.

Dom's jaw twitched, but he was quickly blocked from view by Warren returning. My attention was instantly drawn up to his face, and he smiled down at me.

"Are you ready to leave?"

I tucked my phone back into my purse, picked it up from where it sat by my feet, and stood. "Yep. Are we going in the same direction?"

He offered his address as he touched a hand to my lower back and led me out of the restaurant.

"Not the same," I said, shaking my head.

"Separate Ubers it is," he replied, unperturbed. "Why don't we order, then you can give me your number, and we can plan to meet this week? How about Wednesday night?"

I nodded. "That sounds good to me." I pulled up the app on my phone, ordered my car, and opened my contacts. "Here. Type in your number."

Warren took my phone and typed it in. "What's yours?"

With a grin, I hit dial. His screen lit up with my incoming call, and I hit "End" after a second, and his screen dimmed.

"Smart," he acknowledged. "So, Wednesday? Do you have any preferences?"

"Well, this is my favorite place," I said, gesturing to the restaurant behind us. "So, why don't you pick?"

"Sounds good to me." His eyes sparkled as a black car pulled up against the side of the road. "Is that you or me?"

I checked my phone. It looked like it was mine, but I leaned down just in case.

"Chloe?" The driver with long, bright-blond dreadlocks asked.

I nodded. "Would you give me a second?"

"Sure."

"Thanks." I straightened and turned back to Warren, feeling a little awkward. "Well, thank you. I had a great night tonight."

"Me, too, Chloe." He stepped toward me and, pushing my hair from my eyes, bent his head and gently pressed his lips to mine.

It was warm and comfortable and... nice.

Just nice.

Perfectly, sweetly, nice.

"Yo, lady? Do you want me or not?" The Uber guy knocked on the dashboard, making me jump back from the perfectly nice kiss I'd just shared with Warren.

"Yes," I said, turning to look at my impatient driver. "I'm coming. Now. I'm sorry." I turned to Warren. "I'm sorry. I've gotta go."

"It's okay." His lips pulled to one side. "I think this is mine coming now anyway. I'll call you."

"Okay, sure." I pulled open the back door of my Uber and, when Warren moved toward his, waving goodbye before he turned his back on me, my eyes once again collided with Dom's.

I held his gaze for a second too long before I slipped into the backseat and closed the door behind me.

Surely it had to be the lights of the restaurant glinting off his irises awkwardly, because there was no way Dom was annoyed, was there?

Definitely not at me kissing Warren. He had no reason to be annoyed about that.

Ah, shit.

Had I fucked up? Had I matched him wrong? Was his date bad? Had he had a bad night while I'd had a good time?

And why had that kiss with Warren been nothing more than "nice?"

Was it a learning curve? That happened with new people, didn't it? Like, sex and stuff. It took a while to get used to each other.

Would the kissing get better as we got to know each other more?

Get better.

That was the wrong phrase. He wasn't a bad kisser. In fact, he was a very good kisser. He had lovely, soft lips and applied just the right amount of pressure for a first kiss—one with an audience, too.

It was a lovely kiss, but I just didn't... tingle.

I didn't tingle. There you go. There was no tingle, no fizz, no buzz. No zing of delight as his lips touched mine.

What was wrong with me? Any other single woman would have loved to have had the date I did.

And I had. Loved it. I'd had the best freaking time. He was sweet and funny and hot and someone I could see myself spending a lot of time with.

But what if I never got that zing?

I sighed and leaned back in the seat. There was nothing worse than a great date that had a sour undertone because of no specific reason.

In fact, if anything, having Dom there had been the sour tone. I should have known he'd pick my favorite restaurant for my date. The biggest problem was that it was his, too, and since we operated so similarly when it came to matching people, we'd picked the same place without bothering to talk to each other.

Jesus.

The sooner I was over him, the better.

Let's face it.

The only thing that could make this night worse was getting out of this car and stepping in a pile of dog shit.

Which was, of course, exactly what I did as we pulled up outside my house, I thanked him and got out.

Boom. The heel of my Jimmy Choo went smack in the middle of a pile of dog shit.

Awesome.

***

"He was nice," I said, shrugging and brushing powder off my skirt. Fluffy donut filled my mouth.

Mellie stared at me. "Oh, well, your night went well."

Peyton just tore a bite off her donut and put down her coffee.

"It was good," I said around my food. I quickly swallowed and put down my half-eaten donut. "Look, it was a great first date. It wasn't really awkward or uncomfortable. He was really hot. He's sweet and funny and kind. He has a great career. He lives within forty-five minutes of my place, and I can really see myself spending time with him."

"Okay, aside from the career thing, you sound like you're describing a dog," Peyton said.

She wasn't wrong.

"I know that, but ugh. It's so hard. He's a really, really great guy, and I had a lot of fun—"

"But," Mellie said.

"But nothing." I waved my donut through the air. "This is what I need. I need someone I'm interested in and I can get over that... that... moron next door."

"Oh boy, that was savage," Peyton said flatly. "Chlo, you don't sound enthusiastic about this guy at all."

"I know. But I am. I promise. He's so lovely. He's literally perfect—"

"Which means he probably has a small dick. How big were his hands?"

"I didn't—I mean, I wasn't looking—"

"Isn't it the feet?" Mellie asked, looking between us. "Or is it both?"

Peyton paused. "Generally, it's the ego. Did he have a big one?"

I bit back a giggle.

"Ego, Chloe. Did he have a big ego?"

"Unless she slept with him," Mellie added. "Did you have sex with him on the first date?"

I almost dropped my donut. "No! Oh my God! He kissed me, but—"

"Well? How was it?"

"Nice," I said lamely.

Peyton got up and walked to her desk. She opened a drawer, pulled something out, and walked back over. "Here. Use this. You need it." She threw a book in my lap.

It was a thesaurus. She'd just given me a thesaurus.

"What?" I held it up. "What's this for?"

"You're having a second date, right?"

I nodded.

"When he asks you how you enjoyed your first date, you can't tell him it was nice," Mellie said, pausing to lick powder from her thumb. "It's just that simple, Chlo. Nice is the biggest insult you can give anyone."

"Not true," I fired back. "The biggest insult is 'Is it in yet?'"

"True story!" Peyton said a little too enthusiastically.

"You have experience with that?" I asked, eyebrow raised.

Mellie snorted. "Of course she does. More than we could imagine."

"Here's an idea—fuck yourself," Peyton muttered in her direction.

I laughed. "Okay, back on track, guys. Seriously, Warren is lovely. He's a great guy, and I'm excited to see him again. I really think it's just about me finding someone I'm so interested in that I can't help but get over Dom."

They both paused at that.

Unfortunately, as I said it, it made me sound like a selfishly horrible person.

"Oh God, does this make me a horrible person?" I asked quietly, dropping my half-eaten donut into the box. "Using someone to get over Dom?"

"Are you gonna get under him?" Peyton asked.

"And you're occasionally in charge of a child?" Mellie jerked her head around to look at her. "Peyton!"

"It's a genuine question!" She held out her hands. "And my response depends on her answer!"

Mellie rolled her eyes and looked at me. "Chloe, I'll be honest with you. Yes. It makes you selfish. The only reason you're dating him is to get over the tool next door."

Peyton coughed.

"Oh, he's a tool, and you know it," Mellie said, shooting her a look. "But Chloe, hon, you're not entirely a dick. I mean, you like him. You see potential there. You're interested in getting to know him better. That doesn't make you selfish—that just makes you human. You're not perfect."

"Oh! It's like Monica and Pete!" Peyton clapped her hands together. "You know, she dated him because he was handsome and really nice, but it was only when they parted that she realized she was attracted to him? And that was when she was getting over Richard. Maybe Warren is your Pete."

"Peyton, they broke up," I reminded her.

She waved her hand. "Only because he started fighting. Does Warren look like the fighting type?"

"I don't know. It didn't come up in conversation, funnily enough."

She rolled her eyes. "Fine, fine. But I still stand by it. Even if he's only your stepping stone to getting over my brother, it doesn't matter. Everyone who enters your life is there for a reason, and sometimes that reason is a lesson."

I blinked at her. "Lay off the parenting. You're getting way too philosophical for my liking."

Mellie giggle-snorted.

"I get it, Peyt. Okay? I get it. Thanks. I'll think over my selfishness." I picked my donut back up, and just before I took a bite, I said, "Hey—did Dom mention anything about his date to you?"

She tilted her head slightly to the side and met my eyes. "No. Why? Should he have? I know y'all were at the same restaurant."

"Ouch," Mellie muttered.

"Yeah. We were a few tables away from each other."

"Double ouch," she muttered again.

I waved my hand dismissively in her direction. "He looked like he had a really bad night. Just before we left, he texted me a pretty shit message, and when we were outside, and I was about to get in my Uber, he looked at me like he was ready to kill me."

Her and Mellie shared a look before Peyton shook her head. "No. But I haven't spoken to him, really. Maybe he had a bad date?"

"That's what I thought, but—" I paused, then gave myself a shake. "Hey, we all make mistakes. Maybe I got it wrong for him. It wouldn't be the first time I was slightly off the mark."

"That's probably it," Mellie said. "Not everyone is who they claim on the internet. For instance—our new bar girl? She claims she's a size four with natural blonde hair. Not that I'm judging, but she's a beautiful size twelve with not-so-blonde hair, so maybe his date wasn't all she was cracked up to be."

She was right about that. It wasn't the first time I'd come across a profile from someone who was less than honest.

"It makes sense," I said. "Well, we have a meeting today to talk about it, so I'll ask him."

Another glance passed between my best friends.

"Good idea," Peyton said.

"Yep. Good idea," Mellie echoed.

CHAPTER SIX

DOM

*Turns out, you're not always the fucking saint you think you
are.
Even if your idea of being a saint is deluded.*

TAPTAPTAP.

Taptaptap.

Taptaptap.

That was the sound of my fingers as they beat rhythmically against the solid wood top of my desk. Chloe was coming—I knew she was. I knew she was across the hall with my sister and Mellie, inevitably talking about her date last night.

The date that had gone well.

The date she'd smiled through. The date she'd laughed through. The date she'd enjoyed until the very last second when he'd had to pull away from that goodnight kiss, and she met my eyes.

I'd never loved an Uber driver more than in that moment. I hadn't even meant it. I hadn't meant to be so angry—so furious and agitated, but I hadn't been prepared for it.

Sure. I could take her bright smiles and her melodic laughter as he'd wooed and swooned her. As he'd wined and dined her.

I had to. I had to accept it. I had to push it aside to give my date—what the hell was her name again?—the attention she'd deserved.

That didn't stop the fucking punch in the gut when we'd walked outside, and I'd seen them kissing. Seen him with his hand in her damn blonde hair and her ever-red nails against the blue of his shirt.

Seen his fucking lips on hers.

I had no claim to her. No claim to those glossy, red lips she sported on a daily basis. No claim to her nails creasing my shirt or her eyes roving my body the way hers did to him as he walked to the bathroom.

Fuck.

I shoved myself away from my desk and walked into the kitchen. I wasn't going to get anything remotely productive done while I was this frustrated, so there was no point even trying.

Besides, Chloe was due to get here any second, and I needed to calm down before she got here.

I also needed to remember that she wasn't mine. That Peyton was right. Unless I was willing to be honest and tell her that I had feelings for her, I had no right to feel this way.

I also couldn't tell her. I had to keep reminding myself of that. It was a giant loop of fucking reminders that never seemed to stop.

Why did I have to fall in love with my sister's best friend? The only person in this world I couldn't get along with to save my life?

At this point, I could have a gun to my head, and I still wouldn't be able to get along with her.

I yanked the drip tray from the coffee machine and threw it into the sink to wash out. It clattered, splashing the chrome sides with yesterday's coffee, but I shrugged it off to change out the coffee pod and get the water tank out.

After refilling the water, I gave the drip tray the wash it badly needed and put the machine back together.

Why was I doing this? What did it fucking matter if Chloe hated me? Why didn't I just tell her how I felt? It was blowing up in my face either way, so what did it really matter?

Nothing would change, except her knowledge of my feelings. Feelings I was going to lock away and move on from anyway.

I put my mug under the machine and hit the button. It whirred to life, filling the kitchen with its noise.

I bent forward and grabbed the edge of the counter, dropping my head down. My lips parted as I blew out a long breath, and I briefly closed my eyes.

This was why my sister didn't date until Elliott.

Dating was bullshit. More trouble than it was worth.

"Dominic!" Chloe's yell cut through the final sputter of the coffee machine.

Here we go.

"What did I do this time?" I asked, straightening.

"Why isn't the internet working?"

I turned to see her in the doorway. She stood, leaning against one side, arms folded across her chest. She wore her usual leather jacket, and today it was partnered with light-blue jeans and heeled boots.

And her expression? Well, I'd seen it a million times before.

Wide, angry eyes. A hard-set jaw. Red lips in a firm line.

The hint that she was contemplating my murder.

"Oh. I didn't pay the bill yet." I stirred milk into my coffee and glanced back at her. "Relax. I was going to do it today."

"Why didn't you pay the bill? It's an automatic charge."

Jesus. She really was going to kill me.

"Well, see," I paused. "The business card is missing, so I have to get online and do it."

Disbelief slowly clouded her features, pushing the anger out of her eyes. "You lost the business card? Dom! What the hell?"

"Hey, there's no proof I lost it." I pointed at her. "For all we know, it was stolen." I grabbed my mug and slid past her back into my office.

"Oh, well, thank God for that," she said dryly, turning around to face me. "That's so much better than it potentially being down the back of your sofa."

Yep. Telling her about the stupid feelings I had for her was not a good idea.

"Look, it's fine. I called as soon as I realized yesterday and put a block on it." I set the mug down on my desk. "They're sending another, and it'll be here in a few days."

"You're not reassuring me. If I didn't know you were such a forgetful klutz, I'd say you're deliberately trying to put this business under." She tossed her purse on the chair on the other side of my desk. "When did you lose it?"

Lie. I was going to lie.

"Yesterday. I used it the day before to order printer ink, so it definitely disappeared within a few hours."

That seemed to placate her a little because she looked a little less like a Rottweiler waiting to maul me in the crotch.

"Right. Did you check the account for charges?"

"Going to do that today," I replied. "As well as call the internet company and pay that bill right now, so it gets switched back on."

"Damn right," she muttered. "So, can we use your WiFi?"

"My apartment WiFi?"

"No, your car's."

She was such a fucking smartass.

"No. It's linked with the business account. Peyton's isn't, though."

Chloe did a double-take. "It isn't? It was. We set it up for both offices."

Aw, shit.

I rubbed my hand over the back of my neck. "Yeah, well, she doesn't trust me not to lose the business card where it's registered, so—"

"I can't imagine why." She ground her teeth together again, then paused. Her mouth opened, eyes widening. "Oh my God. This isn't the first time you've lost the card, is it?"

Shit.

Shit, fuck, shit.

"No," I muttered.

"Dominic! Oh my God!" She ran her hand through her blonde hair, dropping her head back with a groan. "I don't know who put you in charge around here."

I cleared my throat. "I'm the oldest. And, technically, I just kind of assumed command around here naturally."

"Why? Because you're the alpha male?"

"Well—"

"The nail on my baby toe is more alpha than you."

I stared at her. "Bank cards are easy to lose. Keys are easy to lose. Maybe I'm too busy making sure that all the business expenses are compiled since you're incapable of printing off a few sheets of paper for online receipts every week."

"Hey!" She jabbed a scarlet-red fingernail in my direction. "There's a big difference between keeping hold of a bank card and a key than email receipts." She pressed three fingers to her forehead and let go a deep breath. "Fine, whatever. It's too early to argue with you, and I woke up late, so..."

I grunted, picking up my coffee and quickly swallowing some of the hot liquid to hide it.

"What was that for?" she asked, dropping her hand and raising an eyebrow. "Did you stay up too late last night or something?"

I knew what she was asking.

Did I fuck—what the hell was her name?—on the first date?

"Not particularly," I replied. "My mood just takes a turn for the worse whenever I see your face."

"Ugh." She waved her hand in my direction and stalked off toward the kitchen.

I smiled behind my coffee as I watched her go.

And to think we still had to have our conversation about how our dates went.

I didn't know if that was a good or bad thing.

***

"All right, let's get this over and done with." Chloe finally emerged from the kitchen twenty minutes later. Moving her purse from the chair to the floor, she sat down and set her oversized Daisy Duck mug on my desk in front of her. "Let's talk about these stupid dates."

I quirked a brow. "Did yours not go well? It didn't look that way to me."

Something flitted across her face, but her expression barely faltered. "It was a perfectly lovely first date," she said, sitting with a poker face.

"Perfectly lovely? Jesus, Chloe. Are you describing a bunch of flowers or a date?"

"It was great." She shifted. "Really. He's a really nice guy, and I'm excited to get to know him better. We're seeing each other this week. That's all there is to it, Dom. You picked well, as much as I hate to admit it."

Not half as much as I hated to hear it.

"Yeah, well," I grunted, shoving my mouse to one side. "I'm good at my job," I muttered, diverting my gaze from her.

Chloe rolled her eyes. "That was never in doubt. I didn't go into business with a clam, did I?"

"Did you just pay me a compliment? It might have been a little backhanded, but I'll take what I can get with you."

"Did you feel me stroke your ego?"

"If you did, it didn't react."

She pursed her lips into a glossy red pout. The annoyance stretched up to her eyes where her brows were slightly turned down, and her gaze belied her annoyance. "Has anyone ever told you how intolerable you are?"

"I tend not to speak with people who don't like me. You are, of course, excluded from that narrative."

"You're intolerable," Chloe continued. "I cannot believe that after a successful date, you still feel the need to piss me off. Never mind James Bond having a license to kill—it's like you have a license to *be* killed."

"Is the license yours?"

"With any luck," she snapped. "Now, cut the shit and tell me how your date went."

"It was perfectly lovely," I said with a smirk.

"If you're not going to take this seriously..."

"I never said I wasn't. I was using the same terminology you used." I leaned back in my chair and crossed my arms. "As far as first dates go, it was a good one. She talked a little too much about herself, but what woman doesn't?"

Chloe's stare was flat and cold. "How the hell does anyone let you match them with an attitude like that?"

I laughed, unmoving. "I was kidding. She was great. Beautiful. She really did talk a bit too much, but whatever. I was too consumed by the way her tits tried to escape from her shirt."

"And here I was, wondering how you made almost thirty years without getting married, you pig," she muttered.

"Same reason you made it twenty-seven years without getting married. It takes a special kind of person to marry an asshole."

"I'll be sure to confirm that with your future wife."

"You can try, but I'm determined you'll never meet her," I shot back. "I'd buy you out of the business before that happened."

She snorted. "Like you could afford my half, Dominic. I match more than you, and you know it."

"If you say so."

"I do. So, are you having a second date with Rachael?"

Rachael. That was her name. Thank fuck she mentioned it.

"Yep," I said. "I'm calling her tomorrow."

Chloe's eyes flitted across my face for a moment before her lips twitched into a smug little smile. "You forgot her name, didn't you?"

"No," I said through a clenched jaw.

That smile grew, and it danced in her eyes. "You're the worst liar ever. Your date went so well you forgot her name."

"I thought it was Raquel. Easy to mix up."

"You're not Paolo, Dom."

"Who the fuck is Paolo?"

"The Italian guy from Friends who calls Rachel, Raquel?"

I shook my head.

She sighed and waved her hand at me. "Whatever. Never mind. So, we're both going on second dates this week?"

I jerked my head in agreement. "With any luck."

"All right. So, we work until then, and we'll get together to see if we're both going on a third."

"Sounds about right."

She picked up her mug and her purse as she stood. "'Kay. I have a meeting with a new client in twenty minutes, so I'll see you later."

I nodded, turning back to my computer. "I have a lunch meeting with a client, so I'll be out of your hair soon enough."

"A lunch meeting?" She paused at the temporary wall we had to separate our offices. "A new client?"

Shaking my head, I barely glanced up at her as I said, "Ruby."

"Ruby?" She coughed, but it sounded a hell of a lot like she was trying not to laugh. "And she can't come here?"

I knew what she was getting at. "No. She's working and doesn't have time to come across the city, so—"

"Sure, she doesn't." She dropped her hand and smirked. "You know the only thing she wants to date is what's inside your pants, don't you?"

"Chloe."

She held up one hand and backed into her office. "All right, all right."

I blew out a long breath and rubbed my hand over my eyes.

Hell, even if Ruby did want what was inside my pants, at least somebody fucking did.

CHAPTER SEVEN

CHLOE

Sometimes, all you need is a lunchtime sangria and donuts.
And by sometimes, I mean all the time.

"WELL." DOM STOPPED IN THE DOORWAY OF MY OFFICE and leaned against the wall—the permanent one. "You were right."

With my lips still pursed around the straw of my sangria, I peered up at him through my lashes.

Did he just—

"Did you"— I said slowly, setting down my Styrofoam cup— "just tell me I'm right?"

"No, I said you were right, not that are you right."

"Semantics." I grinned and sat back in my chair, swinging it side to side gently. "What was I right about?"

He grimaced, swallowing. "Ruby."

Imagine that.

"This is my shocked face." I drew a circle around my face with my fingertip.

I was still grinning. Smugly. Oh boy, was I smug.

"If you're just gonna gloat at me—" Dom pushed off the wall and held up his hands.

"I'm not, I'm not!" Which was easier said than done considering I was trying not to laugh at his expense.

What? I liked being right. Especially when he was the one who was wrong.

He glared at me for a moment.

"What happened?" I asked, picking up my cup to sip again.

Dom opened his mouth, then paused. "Are you drinking?"

"I had a bad meeting. Don't judge me." I put the sangria down. "Don't worry. It's just a small one."

"No judging. I had three shots of vodka after Ruby left."

Wow. And he didn't even drink vodka.

"That bad, huh?"

He ran his hand through his hair. "I wrote off her behavior in our first meeting as her just being a flirty person. I mean, look at her."

"She looked like she charged a hundred bucks for a blowjob, Dom."

"Aren't you, as a woman, not supposed to judge other women?"

"When did I say I was judging her? Hell, if I could get away with charging a hundred bucks for a blowie, I'd take that up in a heartbeat."

"There's this thing called the internet where you can advertise those services, you know."

I gave him a flat stare. "What happened at your lunch 'meeting?'"

"It was a meeting!" He rubbed his hand down his mouth. "It was supposed to be a meeting." He leaned back against the wall again with a sigh. "So, we sat down at our table, got coffee, ordered food, and started talking. I took a folder with a few profile print-outs, so she could narrow down and put me on the right track because she said she was quite fussy."

"Not that fussy if she hit on you." *Says me.*

He flipped me the bird before carrying on. "She narrowed it down to two guys were who pretty similar by the time we were almost done eating, so I was ready to go. We paid, then when we were on the sidewalk, she turned to me and told me she thought I was better looking than those guys I'd given her and kissed me."

"You kissed her?" My eyebrows shot up, even as there was a slightly jealous twang in my chest.

"No. I didn't kiss her. She kissed me," he corrected me. "There's a difference."

"Sure, there is. But did you kiss her back?"

"No!" He balked at my question. "Jesus, Chlo—no, I didn't kiss her back. I pushed her off me and asked her what the hell she was doing."

"She was trying to get into your pants," I pointed out a little too cheerfully. "Like I told you she was."

"I know that now, don't I?"

Laughing, I picked up my cup. "How did you not know that from your first meeting with her? She was all over you. If you were a boat, she'd be a plague-filled rat."

"It looked... different... from my perspective."

"Because you could see down her shirt," I pointed out. "Of course, it was different."

Dom scratched the back of his neck, briefly dropping his eyes to the ground. "Well, yeah. Come on—I'm a guy. Do you think I don't stare at you when you're bending over with a low-cut shirt?"

I blinked at him. "You—you stare at me?"

"When you're bending over with a low-cut shirt," he repeated quickly. "And you happen to be in my line of view. I don't make it a fucking hobby."

Ouch. A simple "yes" or "no" would have sufficed. Hell, even the first half of his answer would have done just fine.

"Whatever," I muttered. "Still, I told you so. She isn't interested in any of the services our company can provide. She's interested in Peyton's."

"Which, thank God, I never signed up for," Dom added.

"What?"

"She tried to get me to be a test subject, but I think I was seeing someone at the time." He shrugged a shoulder. "No big deal."

Right. No big deal.

"Anyway, if you see Ruby in here or she calls, and you answer, tell her I terminated our agreement." Dom stuffed his hands in his pockets.

I scoffed. "Tell her yourself. I'm not your secretary, no matter that she thought."

"You're right." He shrugged once again. "I couldn't have a secretary who looked like you. Or I'd have to make her dress in sweats."

"Dom? Your vodka shots are showing. Shut up."

He grinned. "Anyway. I'm just here to say you're right, and in the future, I'll listen to you."

"Now, I know your vodka shots are showing. Go take a nap upstairs or something."

"That's not a bad idea. Can you call me in an hour to wake me up?"

"Okay, if I'm not your secretary, I'm sure as hell not your keeper. You have an alarm clock on your phone for a reason."

"Phone's dead."

"So? Charge it, numbnuts."

"Numbnuts?" He grinned. "That's a new one."

"I spent too much time reading a hashtag about British insults on Twitter." I shrugged one shoulder. "Here." I opened my desk drawer and pulled out a spare charge cord. "Charger. Charge, set the alarm, sleep. Be an adult, Dominic."

His grin only widened as he took the cord from me. "Thanks, Chlo. You're a doll."

I stared at him. "Really? Three vodka shots and you're calling me a 'doll?'"

He burst out laughing, one hand to his stomach. "No. I'm just fucking with you. But I really did need this cord, so thanks." He raised the lead and winked at me.

And I hated the butterflies that took flight in the pit of my belly.

Fuck them and fuck him.

"Fuck off," I shouted after him.

His laughter echoed in the office as he left, swinging the door shut behind him. A groan escaped me before I stood and pushed back from the stupid wall that separated our offices. The windows on his side of the room were bigger and brighter than mine, and I definitely preferred the natural light over the fake light from the stupid LED bulbs I hated.

Natural light flooded my side of the room. The moving wall looked messy, but since there were no more in-person appointments today, it didn't really matter.

I turned off the overhead light and dropped onto the armchair in the corner of my office. The sun glared at me through the glass, almost burning against my chest, but I didn't care. Weirdly, it felt good.

At least it wasn't in my eyes.

Not that it mattered. I propped my elbow on the arm of the chair and buried my face in my hand.

I needed more fingers if I wanted to count how many times I'd seen Dom with another woman. From high school to today, it was endless. Not because he was a whore, but because he was handsome. And, when he wasn't pissing me off, he was a pretty great guy.

I mean, I wasn't in love with him for his tendency to rub me the wrong way now, was I?

So why did Ruby bother me? Why did Rachael bother me? Why did my stomach feel as though Cupid had taken it and twisted it into a thousand knots?

I was excited to see Warren. But that didn't mean I wanted Dom to see Rachael again.

God, how selfish was I?

No—not selfish. How pathetic was I?

Incredibly. That was the answer. I was hopelessly and completely pathetic. I was a grown-ass woman who needed her neighbor to catch the spiders from her bathtub and who couldn't get over a guy who clearly wasn't interested in her.

Because accidentally looking down my shirt when the opportunity presented itself didn't count.

I let go of a heavy sigh and sat up straight. If only getting over someone was as easy as getting under somebody else.

If that were the case, I'd cross the hall and have Peyton set me up with someone right now.

***

Peyton barked out a laugh. "You don't want me to do that."

"I do!" I smacked my fist against her kitchen table. "I want you to set me up with a hot guy with a big dick who can blow my mind."

Mellie looked between us. "How much has she had to drink?" she asked Peyton.

"Nothing. Which is why I'm concerned," she muttered as a response. The pitcher of margarita she held clinked against the slate mat in the middle of the table when she put it down. "Chloe, you don't want me to set you up with someone. You've never had a one-night stand in your life."

"Twenty-seven seems like a good time to start those," I retorted, grabbing the handle of the pitcher and sloshing the cocktail into my glass. A little splashed onto the table, and Peyton discreetly grabbed a cloth from the sink.

Mellie and I both pretended to look away while the modern-day Monica Geller wiped it up.

"The only thing twenty-seven is good for is binging a new Netflix series," Mellie said, taking the pitcher and pouring her own drink much more precisely than I had. "And don't get a boyfriend, because they will complain that all your suggestions are murder shows."

"Only because he knows you could kill him."

"Which is why one-night stands aren't a good idea. You could also get killed," Peyton pointed out.

"It's all good. I could solve it at this point." Mellie shrugged a shoulder.

I groaned and slumped forward on the table. "I can't do this anymore, guys. I think I have to sell my part of the business."

Peyton spat her drink over the table. Literally all over it—the spray was quite impressive.

Mellie wrinkled her nose and pushed her glass toward Peyton.

"Yeah, yeah, I'll make more," she muttered then turned to me. "No, Chlo. You can't. You can't sell your part of Stupid Cupid just because you set him up with a great woman and he had a two-dollar hooker hit on him."

Obviously. I knew that.

"How ironic. The drama queen of the group is telling one of us not to be dramatic," Mellie mused, cradling her glass in her hand.

Peyton rolled her eyes.

"I just—" I sat back up. "Look, me and Dom are never going to happen. I know that. Accept that. But just because I know we'll never happen, doesn't mean my heart does."

The fickle little bitch.

"I don't know if I can get over him while I'm working with him, that's all," I added as an afterthought.

"So?" Mellie said. "Take a vacation. Take a week off. Two weeks, even. Work from home. Who says you need the office for anything other than a home base to take meetings?"

I hesitated.

Peyton leaned forward, shrugging a shoulder. "You're determined to get over him, so you have to do what you have to do."

Why did that sound so much more ominous than she'd meant it?

CHAPTER EIGHT

CHLOE

Shit happens.
And in my life, men are usually the root cause of said shit.
Well. It's either men or a questionable curry.

WARREN: HEY, CHLOE. SORRY, I CAN'T MAKE IT THIS WEEK. **An emergency came up at work and I'm still out of town. Raincheck?**

Me: Of course. Don't worry about it!

I sighed and set my phone down on the sofa next to me. Working from home had many positives, but also many drawbacks. Like the fact I could pick up my texts instantly because I was almost constantly distracted.

The TV? A distraction. The washing machine? A distraction. A cat walking across my fence outside?

Distraction.

And now I had no plans for the weekend except to work. At least Dom would be out of the office on Saturday evening, so I could catch up on all the things I wasn't doing while sitting at home, on my sofa, browsing social media and watching my Friends boxset from series one, episode one, to the final episode in series ten.

It didn't matter how many times I watched this series. It never got old, and I almost always found something I'd missed before.

This time? It was my dating life.

Another sigh escaped my lips. Nobody ever really said how much it sucked to be the only single one in your group of friends. I couldn't be happier for Mellie and Peyton to have found people they loved and who loved them—and who balanced out their crazy personalities—but that didn't mean I wasn't jealous.

They'd both found their person in the last four months. It was ridiculous to think I'd find mine, too.

Because it sure as hell wasn't the person my heart wanted it to be. And, let's face it, even if it were Dom, it'd be a daily disaster. Between my temper and his skill at losing things, it would be nothing but a hot ass mess.

I pushed my laptop off my legs onto the cushion next to me. The fan whirred to cool it, and the screen blanked off.

How long had I not been working for?

Ugh.

You know what? I was done with this pity party. I didn't even have a ticket to a pity party for one night—I had a freaking season ticket to every party every weekend.

It wouldn't be so bad if I wasn't the only party-goer.

Still, I was done. It was time to make a change. And that started with a new haircut because all good things did.

***

So, as it turns out, I was a big fat chicken.

The new haircut I'd intended to get had ended up with a one-inch trim, meaning the only new thing about my hair was the ends.

I'd take it.

I did get my nails done, though, so there was that. And I felt better. Even with the knowledge that in approximately one hour, Dom would be on his second date with Rachael, and I'd be in the office working like a little loser.

I'd take it. I'd get a pizza on my way to the office and a giant sangria from the cocktail place on the corner of the street.

I pushed my freshly-trimmed bangs out of my eyes and made good on that plan. I grabbed all the things I needed to work for the next few hours, including my laptop, and sent for an Uber. Sangria wasn't exactly the best friend of driving, plus it was Saturday, so if I wanted to get anywhere on time, Uber was the way to go.

Within ten minutes, a shiny, red car pulled up outside my house. Grabbing my things, I headed out, pausing only to lock my front door and tuck my key into my purse.

The Uber guy agreed to stop and wait at my favorite pizza place. The pizza place was, as always, quick to get their stone-baked pizzas out of the oven and into a box, so he wasn't waiting long.

A plus since I'd had to agree to pay him while he waited.

I slid into the back of the car, pizza box in hand, and nodded when he asked if I wanted to go to my final destination now. He seemed relieved at my response and almost pulled out in front of another car as he joined the traffic.

If I was going to die because I stopped for pizza… well, there were worse reasons a girl could die. Carbs were up there with the good ones.

By the time we made it through the Saturday traffic, I was ready to chew my own arm off in hunger. I just about managed to resist, but not without a momentary flash of murderous tendencies thanks to the rude goodbye from the Uber driver.

It wasn't even goodbye. It was a random grunt that said he wanted to be one of the people going to drink instead of driving them around.

Not that I was going out to drink in my yoga pants and sneakers. Nobody did that. Which, really, was a bit of a fucking shame.

The world would be a happier place if a girl could go dancing in her yoga pants.

Think about it; you'd never have to worry about accidentally flashing your panties at a club full of random strangers.

Also, what else would you wear yoga pants for? Everyone knew you didn't actually do yoga in them. You simply wore them like real pants, helping them to fulfill their dreams of one day becoming accepted as real pants.

All right, so that was my dream, but did it matter? For all we knew, all yoga pants everywhere wanted was to be in the same clothing group as jeans.

I snorted to myself as I unlocked the door.

Right. Like yoga pants would ever be equal to jeans.

We all knew they would be far superior.

I put my pizza on a clear corner of my desk and dumped my purse on the floor. I bent to pull my phone out of it and opened up my messages. Going to the thread I kept with the guy who owned the cocktail place on the corner, I hit "New Message."

Me: I found you three more dates.

His response came as quick as lightning.

Luca: On my way.

I laughed and kicked off my sneakers, shoving them underneath the desk. Wiggling my toes, the glitter that adorned my Harry Potter socks winked at me thanks to the light right above my desk.

I crossed my legs on my spinny chair, tucking my feet beneath my thighs. The rich scent of the pizza slammed into me right as the office door opened. I looked up just in time to see Luca swan in. His blue hair was unmissable as it swept across his forehead into green tips.

"I see you dyed your hair again," I said by way of greeting.

"I got bored of the red," he said nonchalantly. "I brought you a little something." He waved a large Styrofoam cup.

"Sangria?" I grinned.

"Of course. That's your working potion. But first…" He held his hand out, palm up, and waved his fingers in a "gimme" motion.

I held up one finger and opened the bottom drawer of my desk. A quick rifle through the files gave me the one I was after, and I grabbed the neon yellow paperclip to pull it out.

"Ooooh!" He put down my drink to clap his hands together. "Tell me about them!"

"Off the top of my head…" I clicked my tongue. "The first guy, Robbie, works downtown at that new gay bar. I can't remember the name—"

"Robbie's."

"All right, so he owns it. I knew he worked there. He's been single for two years, has a pet cat called Rudi, and is looking for something serious."

"Good."

Another click of my tongue. "Number two... I'm not entirely sure about him, but I think it might work for you. He's in his late thirties, so a little older than you usually go for, but he owns one of the most popular ghost tour companies in the city."

"I can go for that." Luca nodded. "What about the last guy?"

I couldn't help but smile. "Oh, he's the cherry on top of everything."

Luca clasped a hand to his chest. "Tell me!"

"Okay." I paused, watching my friend bounce on the spot. "Leo is thirty-two, been single for five years, lives close to downtown, and... moonlights as Cleo four times a week."

He gasped. He didn't breathe out for the longest minute, and I was actually a little afraid he might choke.

"You found me a drag queen?" he finally wheezed. "Oh, honey. You are never paying for another drink ever again."

See? This was a relationship I could get behind.

"Be still my heart," Luca swooned. "Where did you find him?"

"He actually emailed me late last night after his best friend got proposed to on stage at the drag club. I think he'd had a little tequila, but I assured him I had the perfect person for him."

He swayed a little. Actually swayed.

Lord help me if he fainted...

I wasn't equipped to deal with fainting people.

"Screw the others. Email him. I'm gonna date the fuck out of him."

I licked my lips as I tried to come up with a response to that.

Thankfully, his phone rang, saving me the need to carry on down that line that didn't seem to have a light at the end of it.

Luca sighed. "I have to go. Bachelorette parties are out in force, and we found the first of the night."

"First what? Street urinator? Nipple shower? Skirt-tucked-into-panties flasher?"

"Nope. The first should-have-eaten-before-drinking idiot." He rolled his eyes so hard they were millimeters from popping out of his head. "Set me up a date with Leo and text me, okay?"

I picked up my sangria and held it up in agreement that I'd do just that. He left the door to swing shut on its own, and after a sip of the best sangria in the city, I pulled a slice of pizza out of the box.

The door clicked open.

"Was that Luca?" Peyton asked, staring at the cup on my desk.

I nodded, mouth full of pizza.

"And he didn't bring me a drink?"

"D'int know 'oo were 'ere," I said around my dinner.

"Man. I never would have understood that before Briony, but now... got every word." She shook her head in disbelief. "He only ever hand-delivers drinks for a date. What did you pull out of your bag of tricks this time?"

"I didn't even have to pay for it. And the date is so good, I get free drinks forever," I told her, resting my slice back in the box.

Peyton paused. "You didn't."

I nodded, a solemn look on my face. "I found him a drag queen."

"Oh my God. That's only taken, what? Two years?"

"Yep. But, I did it. I found him his dream... man? Woman?" I paused. "What's the correct way to refer to them?"

She frowned. "I think it's him when they're, you know, themselves, and her when they're... well, dressed up."

Where was the real-life Chandler Bing when you needed him?

"Makes sense." I nodded again. "Why are you here late?"

"Late appointments. I'm about to leave. Why are you here?"

"Warren canceled our second date. He's stuck at work out of town." I shrugged a shoulder. "And since Dom is on his second date with Rachael, I figured I could come in and get some stuff done since I'm useless at working from home."

Peyt jerked her head in agreement. "It's hard. But, hey. At least you have, what? Two? Three hours here before he'll get home?"

"Enough time to eat and do what I gotta do."

"You want me to stay and hang out with you for a while?"

"It's okay. We'll just end up streaming Friends on Netflix which would make my trip here counterproductive." I grinned. "But, thanks."

"Okay. In that case, I'm going home to run a hot bath and order pizza since I didn't eat yet." With that, she leaned over the desk and swiped a slice out of my box. "Thanks, love you, bye." She shoved the slice in her mouth before she'd even opened the office door.

I glared at her back, but I couldn't help smiling.

Hey—I felt like crap, but tonight, I'd made someone happy. And that was what my job was about.

Making people happy.

Even if I struggled to find happiness myself sometimes.

***

"Chloe!"

My name was a faint cry thanks to the headphones in my ears. I pulled one out and looked up, jumping when I saw it was Dom.

"Jesus, Dom. What are you doing here?" I asked, pressing my hand to my chest.

"I was going to ask you the same question. It's nine o'clock on a Saturday night. Are you working?"

I nodded. "I had nothing else to do, so I thought I'd get some work done."

He rubbed his hand across his forehead. "I have questions."

"I have leftover pizza," I offered.

"Leftover pizza? Can't have that." He pulled my client chair out so he could sit down and reached for the closed box.

"Don't get too excited," I said, pulling out the other earbud and pausing Shawn Mendes. "There are only two slices left."

"Pizza is pizza," he said, folding one slice in half and shoving it into his mouth like a savage. "Eye 'oo 'orkin'? 'At abou' date?"

I assumed that meant, "Why are you working? What about your date?" in the highly challenging language of English.

"Warren had to cancel yesterday. Got caught up with some work stuff out of town, so we took a raincheck." I shrugged the same way I had when I'd told Peyton. "Why are *you* here? Aren't you supposed to be on your date? Or are we living parallel lives where we both get canceled on?"

Dom laughed, shaking his head. "Nah, I've already been on it."

I blinked at him for a minute. "You said it was nine."

"We had dinner. Who eats dinner at nine at night?"

I waved my hand at him finishing my pizza.

"No. Not dinner. This is a snack." He held up the folded slice as if to emphasize his point. "I already had dinner. A snack, Chloe. A very tasty snack."

"All right, I get it. It's a snack. But that doesn't explain why you're here."

"Do you want a play-by-play of the whole night?"

Couldn't think of anything worse, if I was honest. "Not particularly. I just think you're back early."

"We got done with our first date about this time."

I rolled my eyes. "First dates are a different story." I finished the last of my sangria and threw the cup into the trashcan. "They're supposed to be shorter. You're getting to know each other. Second dates should just be... longer. I don't know. Eat dinner and then go dancing—"

"I don't dance," Dom said firmly.

"Lies. I've seen you do the Macarena."

"Only because I lost a bet to Peyton when I was fifteen. She deliberately requests that song at all our family get-togethers."

It was true. I couldn't remember the details of the bet, but I remember him being stupidly confident that he wouldn't have to do the Macarena at every party ever, and that he'd be able to revel in smugness as he made his sister do it.

"Okay, but that's still funny." I fought a smile.

"I don't dance by choice," he corrected himself. "Is that good enough?"

"It'll do. Still, you could have gone for a walk, grabbed a coffee, a cocktail to walk through the square with…"

Dom sighed and put down the last slice of pizza. "What are you getting at?"

"Nothing!"

"You fish any harder and you're gonna reel in a goddamn shark," he grumbled.

"I'm just saying that you're home early from your date." I held out my hands. "If something went wrong, you may as well tell me. You're going to have to eventually."

"It didn't go wrong. It was just a short date."

"No, a short date is coffee in a lunch hour."

"You're really starting to get on my nerves, Chloe."

Good. He was getting on my nerves, too. It wasn't like I hadn't noticed how well that white shirt hugged his upper body, stretching over his biceps whenever he bent his arms.

For crying out loud, the material was going to rip if he kept doing it.

And I wasn't even going to go there with the rolled sleeves. Nuh-uh. No way, Jose. Not a chance, rain dance.

Maybe it was the sangria, but I kinda wanted to lick the veins on his forearm.

Yep. It was the sangria.

I propped my chin up on my hands. "Am I? I couldn't tell."

CHAPTER NINE

DOM

Not all women were sugar and spice and all things nice.
Some were just spice.
Or maybe that was just Chloe after sangria.

"ARE YOU DRUNK?" I RAISED AN EYEBROW AT HER.

She shook her head, still keeping it propped up on her hands. "Luca makes a mean sangria, but I've been sipping that one so long it was basically lukewarm." She wrinkled up her face, her makeup-free skin showing a light dusting of freckles that she usually kept covered up. "Unless being drunk would make you tell me why you're here so early..."

"It was just a short date. What else do you want me to tell you?" I got up and walked toward the kitchen.

"You're so full of shit, Australia can smell you."

"Well, they're welcome. I smell good tonight." I chuckled to myself and turned on the kitchen light.

"You're so annoying," Chloe muttered.

"Says the one annoying me," I shot back over my shoulder.

God, the woman could drive a man to drink himself into a grave. There was nothing about this date I wanted to share with her. I could say that with one hundred percent certainty.

Not because Rachael and I weren't compatible, and she'd gotten it wrong, but because I didn't want her to go and be with Warren if I didn't have anyone. That was the whole point of this exercise—to get over her. Maybe seeing her with someone else would work, but before it did, it'd fucking hurt.

"I just want to know what happened. We said we'd check in, so check in."

"I don't want to." I turned around and met her eyes.

She stared at me, folding her arms across her chest. She was makeup free aside from a tiny lick of mascara on her eyelashes, and that was a strange sight in itself.

Not that I didn't love it.

I did.

I thought she was fucking beautiful when she wasn't hiding all the things that made her, her. The freckles that lightly dusted her nose. The tiny mole at the edge of her left eyebrow. The chickenpox scar right next to her ear.

"What went wrong, then?" she demanded. "Do you just not like her? I can find you someone else if that's—"

"She's a great person," I cut in before she could carry on. "I like her just fine."

"Just fine? Are you describing your date or the dessert?"

"Chloe. Drop it." I turned back to the coffee machine.

I didn't want to tell her that her client had lied on her application. I didn't want to tell her that she'd omitted a huge part of her life when she'd filled out all the information.

If she'd put it in, there was no way Chloe would have ever matched her with me.

"I just want to know. It's not about you. If I've done something wrong in matching you—"

I spun on the balls of my feet and took one step to close the space between us. She drew in a deep breath, her lips parting with the sharp inhale.

"I said" —my gaze met hers— "drop it."

There was a flash of surly defiance in her eyes. One that closed her lips and made them press into a thin line. Her brows drew together like she was plotting my death within seconds of me speaking.

She was fierce.

And it was my favorite thing about her.

"I won't drop it," she said stubbornly. "Not until you tell me what happened."

"Why do you care so much?"

"I clearly made a bad match. It's my job to match you with the person that's best for you."

Which was something she couldn't do.

The bare-faced fact of the fucking matter was that it would never happen.

None of the people she could ever match me with would be good enough.

None of them would ever be her.

I gripped the doorframe, one hand on either side and held her gaze steady. "She lied on her application and admitted it to me tonight. Nothing you could have done would have made a difference. On paper, she was perfect. In real life, not so much."

Chloe ran her tongue over her bottom lip, and fuck if my eyes didn't flick to the smooth sweep of it.

"Now, will you drop it?" I asked, dipping my head down to her.

She swallowed but shook her head just the tiniest amount. "What did she lie about?"

"Jesus fuck, Chlo." I pushed off the frame and ran my hands through my hair. "You're killin' me over here."

"I just want to know! Do I need to do more in-depth research? I mean—"

"She has a fucking kid!" I threw my arm out to the side.

She froze, mouth open where I'd interrupted her.

"Yeah," I said a lot quieter. "She has a child, and I'm the asshole who told her we couldn't see each other again because I'm not ready to have a child in my life."

I wasn't my sister. I didn't have any lingering feelings the way she'd had with Elliott. I wasn't ready to have a child of my own, never mind anyone else's.

"That doesn't make you an asshole," Chloe said. She looked down at her hands, fidgeting. "If anything, she's the asshole."

I folded my arms and raised an eyebrow. "How do you figure that?"

With a tiny shrug of her shoulder, she said, "She didn't tell you she had a child. She deliberately lied on her profile. I mean, come on. She has a child. It's not like she has five cats and a pet llama in the backyard."

I snorted. I couldn't help it. "A pet llama?"

"Hey, I've seen it before. Or maybe it was an alpaca? I don't know. They look the same." She waved it off. "Point is, she kept major information from her profile. You're not a horrible person for not seeing her again when she's someone you should never have been matched with in the first place."

"Yeah? Can you tell her that? She looked at me like I was the physical embodiment of Satan."

Chloe perched on the edge of my desk. "That's probably just because she could see right through you."

"He clearly changed his host from you to me, then."

She grinned. "Nah, I was just temporary. You were always his favorite."

I let out a small laugh. "Whatever. But now you know, so you can leave me alone."

"Do you want me to find you another date? I have a couple still from when I—"

"No."

"No?" She opened and closed her mouth a couple times. "No?"

"No," I repeated, just as firmly. "Thank you, but no. I don't want you to find me another date."

"Why not?"

"Because I don't want one." I held my hands out to my sides. "It's that simple, Chlo. I'm good for now."

She stood up off the desk and walked over to me. "But, how—"

I let out a heavy sigh and grasped her shoulders. I made sure I met her eyes before I spoke because I wanted her to know that I was being completely serious.

"Chloe," I said softly. "I don't want you to find me another date. Not that Rachael wasn't great until the whole 'I have a daughter' thing, but because I just don't want one."

She dropped her gaze to my left arm briefly before bringing her eyes back up to mine. "Why not?"

"Because, and I mean this in the nicest way possible when I say this—"

"I don't like the sound of this."

"—Nobody you match me with will be able to compare to what I really want, all right?"

Her lips parted, but she didn't say anything.

"So, it's just that simple," I finished. "I don't want to date anyone right now."

"I don't understand," she said softly.

"You don't need to understand. It's my issue, not yours." I dipped my head once again, so our faces were close. "So, leave it now. All right? Focus on the people who need your help to find a date, because I don't see myself being one of them anytime soon."

"I don't—" she stopped before she presumably repeated herself. "But you were all for this before. What changed your mind?"

Sitting across from another woman and comparing everything about her to you.

"I don't think I was ever really into it," I admitted. "Not like you are."

"Oh." Her expression dropped slightly. "I guess—okay, fine."

"Fine? You're not going to argue with me?" I dropped my hands from her upper arms and took a step back. "Wow. Okay." I gave her a quick once-over and stopped.

She looked different—aside from no makeup.

Chloe lifted a hand to her face. "What? Is there something on my face? In my hair?" She ran her fingers over her cheeks and then through her hair.

Her hair.

"Did you cut your hair?" I asked, squinting slightly.

"Oh. That. Yeah. Just a bit." She blushed and tucked it behind her ear. "Why? Does it look bad?"

You could be bald, and the answer would still be no.

"No," I said honestly. "You look great."

She froze, as if she thought I'd tell her otherwise. Her cheeks flushed pink. "Oh. Thanks."

"You're welcome." I tugged my lips up to one side. "I'm gonna go upstairs. Can you lock up?"

"Sure. I'll see you Monday?"

I pulled open the office door and with a glance over my shoulder to the woman who was still blushing, nodded. "See you Monday, Chlo."

CHAPTER TEN

DOM

Love was fucked up.
So was honesty.
Who wanted to risk a punch in the balls just to be a good
person?

"FUCK."

I let go of my cock and rested my forehead against the cold tiles of my shower.

Waking up with a boner and jerking off to the thought of my sister's best friend wasn't how I planned to start my Sunday.

It wasn't how I planned to start any day if I was honest. I'd done it a few too many times over the past several years, to the point I was now standing here, wondering if I was in love with her or obsessed with her.

Were they one and the same? Interchangeable? Polar opposites?

Could they be mutually exclusive? Was there a healthy way to be obsessed with somebody?

I didn't think there was, but if there was, I was living it. I didn't stalk her, I didn't hound her, and I did everything in my power to ignore how I felt about her.

All for her.

Because, fuck.

Getting over Chloe Collins was a mountain the size of Everest, and I wasn't sure I was able to climb it.

The hot water beat down on my upper back, literally breaking down the stress I held in my shoulders. I rolled my shoulders back a couple times until the dull ache had gone.

Then slapped my hand against the tiles and pushed off them. Water smacked me in the face, and I rubbed my left hand over it before stepping out of the water to grab the sponge.

What the fuck was I doing with my life? Standing in the shower lamenting my lack of self-control like I was a teenage boy?

I needed to get a grip. I also needed a distraction. Work was the best possible one at my disposal, so that was how I'd spend my day.

I finished soaping off and got out of the shower. After quickly drying my hair, I wrapped the towel around my waist and headed for my room. Since it was Sunday, I knew Chloe wouldn't be around the office.

I dried off quickly and tugged on some sweatpants. Droplets from my hair dripped down my back, and I smacked at the back of my neck to stop any more from falling as I made my way downstairs.

I stopped only to grab my phone and keys, then headed down to the office. It was dark and deathly quiet, almost eerie. The flick of the light switch echoed through the empty room as the bulb blinked to life.

Thank God for that.

I blew out a breath and walked over to my desk. While my laptop loaded, I went to make a coffee.

A search in the fridge said we were out of milk.

Fuck it.

I stared at the coffee being poured. I could drink it black, or I could not be damn lazy and go upstairs to my apartment to get the milk out of my own fridge.

I groaned, but ultimately, there was only one option. I wasn't drinking fucking black coffee.

I took the stairs two at a time to my apartment, grabbed the milk from my fridge, and went back down. My coffee was done pouring, so I finished fixing it up and took a seat at my desk.

I had a list of matches as long as my arm to look at, so I signed into my laptop and pulled the first file from the pile of printouts to my left.

Christine Smith. Twenty-eight. Bartender. Lived in Baton Rouge. Looking for a guy between the ages of twenty-eight and thirty-five who lived within one hour of her address, liked food and hiking, and didn't watch sports all the time.

Trust me to pick up the hardest one first.

I huffed out a breath and opened the program. Entering her information and wants would log all the potential matches on our system, and I'd just have to go through them to weed out any that I didn't think would work. The keyword software simply took the hardest part out of it.

Besides, there were thousands of applications on this website. There was no way one person—hell, even ten people—could get through this one by one.

I sat back, tapping my fingers against the arms of my chair as the software loaded through. Names appeared on a list at the side of my screen, and it quickly reached one hundred. I pulled more keywords from her profile and, when the software was done with the first round, I input those for it to match to the one hundred and thirty-one names it'd spat out minutes ago.

It narrowed it down to forty. Much easier to go through personally. I saved the search and downloaded all the profiles to my laptop to get ready to go through.

The office door clicked open.

I froze, my gaze darting upward.

"What are you doing here?" Chloe asked, standing in the doorway.

I relaxed. "Working. Why are you here?"

"Left my phone here last night." She shut the door behind her and walked to her side of the room. She re-emerged seconds later, her phone tight in her hand. She waved it awkwardly. "What are you working on?"

"I've got some matches that have been sitting here a while," I said, focused on the screen instead of her. She looked fucking gorgeous in her trademark leather jacket, white tank, and ripped jeans. The last thing I wanted was to be distracted by her when the whole reason for me being here was to focus on something else.

"Oh. Fair enough. How many do you have?"

I shrugged a shoulder and glanced at the pile. "I think there's around six."

"So, you'll be here all day?"

I nodded.

"Dom… are you all right?"

"Why wouldn't I be?" I asked, disregarding one of the matches the system had thrown out. He played sports, so there was no way he wouldn't watch it all the time.

"You just seem… weird," Chloe said. "For one, you're working half naked."

"Well," I said, clicking on another profile, struggling to keep my eyes trained on the screen, "I wasn't exactly expecting you to come by, or I'd be wearing a shirt."

"You don't—I mean…" she trailed off, then coughed.

I peered over the top of the screen, one eyebrow quirked in amusement.

"Don't wear a shirt on my account," she said. "I'm just here for my phone."

"Just as well. I don't have one down here." I smirked and looked back at the computer.

"Right. Why would you?"

I saw her shift awkwardly out of the corner of my eye.

"I was going to ask you something, but I guess that can wait until tomorrow."

I finally pushed the laptop away and looked up at her. "Why can't you ask me it now?"

"Because you're—" She swallowed, blushing. "Never mind."

"Because I'm shirtless?" I smirked.

"I didn't say that."

"You were going to."

"You can't prove that." She folded her arms across her chest, eyes flashing in challenge.

"I don't need to, Chlo. You're blushing like a thirteen-year-old who just met the eyes of the high school quarterback."

She clapped her hands to her cheeks and pursed her lips. "Now, I'm not going to ask you because you're pissing me off."

Laughing, I waved my hand, then leaned back in my chair. "Just get on with it. I have work to do."

She hesitated for a second, as if she were really considering leaving. "I was thinking about what you said yesterday." She walked to my desk and put down her phone and keys. "About not wanting a date?"

"If you're asking whether I've changed my mind, the answer is still that I haven't."

"No." She gripped the back of the chair on her side of the desk and leaned forward, just slightly allowing me a look down her shirt at her cleavage. "I was thinking about what you said after. About anyone I find not being able to compare to what you want."

I didn't like where this was going. I should have just agreed to a new date, shouldn't I? Fuck it.

"What about it?" I ran my tongue over my teeth.

"What did you mean when you said that?"

I tilted my head to the side. "Why did it have to mean anything? Can't I have an idea of the kind of woman I'd like to date?"

She shifted, one shoulder rolling back as she straightened up. "Well, yeah. Sure, you can. I mean, I have an idea of the kind of guy I want to date. I was just... you sounded specific."

"I would hope I did. Otherwise, my idea of the woman I'd like to date is just a hair color and the fact she has a pair of tits." I drained the last of my coffee and got up. Her eyes followed me as I walked to the kitchen, mug in hand. "Are you checking me out, Chloe?"

"No!" she shouted a little too loudly. "I was just... watching you go and thinking that you're lying."

"Ah, lying." I put the mug in the sink and leaned against the doorframe, grinning at her. I folded my arms. "There's some of that going around today."

Her gaze dropped first to my arms, then to my lower stomach.

I cleared my throat. "You're doing it again."

"Oh my God, put a shirt on!" she snapped. "Walking around like that, you're basically asking me to stare at you like you're a piece of meat!" She flung her arm in my direction, running her other hand through her hair.

My cheeks hurt I was grinning so much. "I don't have a shirt. I told you that. You'll just have to behave until this conversation is done. Unless, of course, you want to leave."

"I want you to tell me what you meant when you said what you did. I can help you find—"

I shook my head. "No, you can't help me. It's done, Chloe, give up. I don't want to date anyone right now."

"But—"

"There are no buts!" I pushed off the frame and stared her down. "No buts. I don't want to date. I don't want you to find me a date. It'll happen when it happens. Shouldn't you be worrying about your own date instead of what I'm doing with mine?"

"He's still out of town." Another awkward shuffle.

"So, you're fixating on me now?"

"If you'd put a shirt on, I wouldn't have to."

I laughed. "I'm not putting a shirt on. Just like I'm not gonna put any underwear on."

She dropped her eyes to my crotch.

I cleared my throat once again.

"For the love of God!" Chloe clapped her hand over her eyes and spun around.

More laughter escaped me. "Someone needs to get laid."

"Someone needs to dress to see other people," she hissed.

"Excuse me if I wasn't expecting you to come by today."

"It's my office, too!"

"I know. I have to listen to you bitch at me at least five days a week." I walked back over to my desk. "Now you've gotten your phone, are you gonna leave me in peace to work?"

"No. Maybe I'll stay and work, too," she shot back defiantly.

Just to be a pain in my fucking ass.

"Why? Do you wanna stare at me some more?"

Her jaw dropped, making her lips form a little 'o'.

"I get it. It's not bad, is it?" I motioned to my body. "I work for these abs. They're too good to be kept under a shirt. Look away, Chloe."

Her eyes darted across my body once more before she glared at me.

At my face.

"You're so full of yourself. No wonder you're single. Nobody could put up with your egotistical bullshit," she snapped.

"You're the one who keeps staring at me and feeding the ego, babe."

"If you call me babe again, I'm going to shove my fist down your throat."

"If you don't get distracted by my stomach on your way."

She set her jaw, her eyes flashing with frustration as she stared at me. "I hope you find the girl you're determined is so perfect and she wants to twist your cock off with a rusty wrench when she realizes how much of an insufferable human being you are."

I already found her.

And I'm pretty sure the wrench thing came from the heart just then.

"Shouldn't be too difficult," I told her. "I already met her, and I'm pretty sure she feels that way."

She did a double-take, blinking furiously at me. "You already met her? Is that why you won't let me set you up with anyone?"

"No, I won't let you set me up with anyone because I don't want to go out with anyone. How many more times do I have to say that?"

"Until you can say it convincingly enough for me to believe you! I can't believe you've already met someone and you let me set you up in the first place!"

"It's never gonna happen!" I threw my arms out. "All right? Me and her are never gonna happen because she doesn't know, and I'm not going to tell her."

"Why not?"

"Well, for one, she hates my guts."

She rolled her eyes. "Can't imagine why."

"For two, she's seeing someone else. Someone I set her up with."

She gasped. "It's a client? Your ideal woman is a client?"

I shrugged a shoulder. I couldn't clarify it to her. If I said yes, she'd do her best to find her. If I said no...

She'd probably figure out I was talking about her.

"Doesn't matter. Give it a rest, okay?" I ran my hand through my hair. "It's not gonna happen."

"How do you know it won't happen? You don't know unless you try."

"Because I know. I just do."

She folded her arms. "I think you should try."

"I think you should give it a rest." I met her eyes and walked over to her. "Seriously, Chloe, drop it. I don't want to talk about this anymore."

"Why not?" She stared up at me, eyes shining with frustration. "Just tell her how you feel. It's not a big deal."

"It is to me. All right? It's a fucking big deal to me."

"Dom, your job is literally matching people up. If she's the person you think you should be with, why don't you just say it?"

I rubbed my hand over my face. "I'm not telling her. Why is that so fucking hard for you to understand?"

"Because I don't get it! If she'd make you happy, just tell her!"

"It's not going to happen! She hates me."

"So should every woman in her right mind! My God, Dom. Grow a pair and fucking tell her how you feel!"

My stomach tightened in knots.

She wasn't going to let this go.

I'd backed myself into a corner, and there was only one way out.

"You want me to tell her?" I turned around to face her, meeting her eyes.

She nodded. "If she's got you this fucked up, you have to."

"Fine. I'll tell her."

"Okay, good." She shuffled, dipping her chin and looking at the ground.

My heart thumped in my chest as I crossed the room. The distance between us closed in seconds, and Chloe looked up right before I stopped in front of her.

"What are—"

I cupped her face and kissed her.

She froze.

And so did I.

We stood in the middle of the office, my hands on her face, lips together, neither of us moving save for taking a breath.

Then, she leaned into me. Her fingers ghosted across my waist as she moved onto her tiptoes.

And I lost all self-control.

I dove my fingers into her hair, holding her right against me as I deepened the kiss. She tasted of cinnamon and sugar, and I knew that she'd had donuts for breakfast.

Her hands slid up to my waist, and she dug her fingers into my skin as my tongue flicked against her lips.

I wanted more. I wanted to taste her more, kiss her harder, bring her closer to me.

I slipped one hand out of her hair and down her back, pulling her body flush against me. Her hand ran up my arm and cupped the side of my neck, and she parted her lips, touching my tongue with the tip of hers.

I pushed her back against the wall, breaking the kiss only for a second to make sure I didn't push her against the door. The second her ass hit the wall, I kissed her again. She tilted her head back, her nails digging into my skin.

My pulse thumped, sending blood rocketing through my veins and straight down to my cock. The more I kissed her, the harder I got, and the more I wanted her.

I'd spent years wondering what it'd be like to kiss her, and now I was doing it, it was fucking beyond anything I'd ever cooked up in my imagination.

I wanted to kiss her until I couldn't breathe. Until I could hear nothing but my pulse thundering in my ears. Until there was nothing but Chloe consuming every inch of my body.

I could kiss her for-fucking-ever.

She slowly broke her lips away from mine, dipping her chin so that her nose grazed across my jaw. Her breaths were unsteady, and they fanned across my collarbone.

She didn't move, and neither did I.

I'd just kissed her.

And she'd kissed me back.

That wasn't how it was supposed to happen—she was supposed to push me away, hell, she could have even hit me, and I wouldn't have cared.

"You just kissed me," she whispered, lifting her head and meeting my eyes.

I took a deep breath and nodded. "Yeah. I did."

"Oh, my God." She pulled her hands from me and covered her mouth with them. Her eyes were wide, shining with confusion and—fuck, want.

The same desire that coursed through my body as I tried to calm my own breathing was the same one I saw reflected back at me in her gaze.

"I can't—I have to—go." She slid away from me, walking briskly to the desk. She snatched up her phone and keys and all but ran out of the office without looking at me again.

The door clicked shut, leaving me in silence.

"Fuck," I whispered, resting my forehead against the wall.

Fuck.

CHAPTER ELEVEN

CHLOE

My mom always told me to expect the unexpected. I've always thought she meant expect your period at random times of the day.
Not for your best friend's brother to kiss the shit out of you.

I AMBLED OUT OF THE MAIN DOOR OF THE BUILDING AND onto the sidewalk, almost walking into a man in a suit. He shot me a dirty look, and I babbled an apology.

Dom kissed me.

Dom. Kissed. Me.

My lips still tingled from where he'd moved his across mine, and the lingering taste of coffee still overwhelmed my senses.

Oh, God.

What did I do now? Where was I supposed to go? How did I begin to think about what had just happened?

I was at the office. Mellie's hotel was two blocks away. I'd go there.

She had alcohol there.

And I needed something to calm my nerves.

I walked, swerving in and out of the happy, laughing people on the sidewalk. My heart was thumping so hard I couldn't hear a damn thing as it echoed in my ears. All I could do was focus on putting one foot in front of the other to get to the hotel.

Why had he kissed me?

There was no way I was the person he was talking about. The one who was his standard for any other woman. It didn't make sense—we were oil and water. How could I possibly be the one who nobody else measured up to in his eyes?

Was it possible we were both harboring feelings for one another? Had he allowed me to set him up originally for the same reason I'd had him set me up?

To move on? To get over him?

Was he trying to get over me?

He couldn't do that. I didn't even know he was under me.

This was too much information to process. I was still running on a high of the feeling of his lips against mine, of our bodies being pressed to each other, of how it felt that moment when it clicked that he was kissing me.

Euphoria.

It was a flash of pure euphoria.

I pushed open the hotel door and stepped into the cool lobby. The cold air felt good as it prickled against my skin. The hairs on my arms stood on end as I moved through the lobby to where a new girl was manning the reception desk.

"Hi," I said, leaning on the desk. "Is Mellie around?"

She peered over from her computer with a bright smile. "Can I ask why you need to see her?"

That was new.

"I just need to speak with her," I said in my own best customer service voice.

"I'm not sure she's available."

A shadow fell over the desk. "Did you see a ghost?"

I looked over and up at Jake. "No, but I may as well have."

"You look like death," he noted.

"I feel like I might be on the brink of it," I admitted.

He nodded his head. "Come on. Mel's on the phone, but you can go back. Do you need anything?"

"Something alcoholic."

"I never assumed otherwise." His eyes twinkled with laughter. "Go on. I'll bring you a drink. Erica, a moment?" he directed the last part to the girl behind the reception desk.

She went deathly white. "Yes, sir."

"Just a note," Jake said, lips twitching. He winked at me.

I smiled and skirted out to the staff door. I punched in the code in the newly-added lock system, and it beeped, clicking to let me through. I pushed it open and walked down the hall to where I heard Mellie's voice before I saw her.

"No," her voice echoed through the ajar door. "I'm not willing to accept that, Jonathan. This is the third order y'all have messed up in the past three months. We're not running a joke here; we're running a successful hotel. Either y'all fix this and get us the missing items on our order in the next twelve hours, or I'll be contacting the bank for a partial refund and finding another supplier who won't let us down every four weeks."

Wow.

I rapped my knuckled against the door lightly and poked my head through.

She looked up from where she was sitting at her desk and motioned me to come in. "That's what I thought. I want the missing portion of the order at the back door by eight a.m." She hit the button on the phone and put it back on the dock. "Hi! What's—" Her gaze settled on me, and her brow creased. "Hey," she said, standing. "What's wrong?"

I swallowed, clasping my hands in front of my stomach. It was still in knots, and my throat felt as though it was closing up.

"Chlo?" Mellie rounded the desk to me.

"Dom kissed me."

Her eyes widened. "He did what?"

I swallowed, desperately trying to wet my now-dry throat. "He kissed me."

She pressed her hand to her mouth before quickly dropping it. "Like a kiss, or a *kiss*?"

"A *kiss*!" I fisted my hair with both hands. "Like a kiss, Mel. A real kiss."

Her lips parted. "What the—why? What did he do that for?"

"I don't know!" Still with my hair entangled between my fingers, I pressed my hands against my burning cheeks. "Last night, he said he wasn't going to have another date with Rachael because she lied about being a single parent on her profile—"

"Oh, this sounds good." Jake slid into the office behind me and pushed a sangria into my hand. "And this. Tequila. Clearly for your nerves."

I took the tiny shot glass of clear liquid and tossed it back without a second thought. My chest was already constricting, and I didn't want to get any tenser than I already was.

"Thanks." I handed him back the glass and sat in his office chair.

"Welcome." He half-smiled. "What's going on?"

"Dom kissed her," Mellie said so I didn't have to. "And on purpose."

"Aside from the fact you said that like you're fifteen and sharing it with a group of girlfriends on the phone," Jake said with one eyebrow quirked, "I caught something about a lie about being a single parent, and I find myself woefully interested in this whole situation."

"You're aware we set each other up?" I asked, stirring my drink with the straw.

He nodded and perched on the desk.

"My guy is away for work, but he had his second date last night. I was working and turns out, she lied on her stuff and has a daughter. That's not something Dom is interested in, so..." I shrugged a shoulder. "I wanted to set him up with someone else, but he said no. Said there was someone he'd always compare them to and after a bit of a fight—"

"You trying to get it out of him," Mellie snorted.

"—I gave up and he went to bed," I continued. "But this morning, I realized I'd left my phone at the office, so went by to get it. He was working, and I asked again."

She shook her head. "Of course, you did."

"Hey, look!" I waggled my finger at her. "I thought about it last night in the bath and figured that if this mystery woman was the bar he was using to score all others against, she had to be pretty special."

Jake smirked.

"So, when I was there this morning, I made my point. If she was that big of a deal to him, he had to tell her. We went back and forth—"

"You fought like hell," Mellie corrected me, earning herself a nod of agreement from Jake.

"We fought like hell," I reluctantly agreed. "I think I pissed him off enough that he finally agreed to tell 'her,' and the next thing I know, he kisses me."

Jake let go of a long, low whistle. "Plot twist."

"Not really. She started with that." Mellie flashed him a grin, then turned to me. "Well? What happened then?"

"I kissed him back," I said simply. "So, we kissed, then I realized what was happening, and I ran away."

"Of course you did." She smiled. "And came here?"

"I panicked. I still can't make sense of it. All that, and he kisses me?"

Jake scratched the back of his neck. "What can't you make sense of, Chlo? So, he has this woman he holds higher than anyone you could ever match him with, but he won't tell you who that is or anything about her. You get to him enough that he agrees to tell her, and he kisses you. That's pretty cut and dry from where I'm sitting."

"Honey, she's been in love with him for ten years. If this situation were cut and dry, she'd have lost her virginity to him on prom night instead of Alex Dupre."

"Hey! Stop telling everyone that!" No matter that she had a point. "I get what you're saying, okay? But it doesn't make sense. How can I be that person to him? We don't get along at all."

Mellie walked back around the desk and sat in her chair. "Well, he's that person to you, isn't he?"

"No. I want to marry someone who is capable of keeping hold of their keys without losing them for longer than two weeks. I want someone who's reliable and steady and doesn't need their hand to be held because they're a mess. I already have you and Peyton for that."

"Hey!"

Jake cough-snorted into his hand. Except it was a little more snort than a cough, and that didn't work out well for him. He ended up actually coughing and smacked his fist against his chest to clear it.

Mellie shot him a dark look. "I don't mean his stupid parts. I'm sure there are lots of things about you that piss him off—"

"Like what?"

"Well," Jake said croakily. "As the third party here—Mellie, honey, you're a hot mess, and she's right. Between you and Peyton, she doesn't need another adoptee on that train," he said to her. "And, Chloe? Darlin', don't take this the wrong way, but you can be difficult to get along with."

My jaw dropped. "How so? I'm the nicest of all of us!"

"I am inclined to agree with you in general there," he said warily, shooting Mellie a look, "But you have your moments. Sometimes you're a little... uptight."

"Uptight?"

Mellie grimaced.

"You're just... you're strung quite tight." He was looking like he regretted opening his mouth. "I don't mean that in a bad way. It's part of your personality. Like how Mel's clumsy as fuck and Peyton is a little OCD about things."

"I'm not clumsy," she grumbled.

Even I scoffed at that. It was a wonder she could do her mascara every day without poking herself in the eye.

"So, Mellie's clumsy, Peyt's OCD, and I'm uptight?" I clarified.

Jake swayed. "Not in a bad way. You're just... fFuck how do I say this? Particular? No. Shit."

I stared at him.

"I think what he's trying to say is you're put together. Out of all three of us, you're the one who, in general, has your shit together," Mellie interjected. "And given how useless we are, that makes you uptight." She shrugged a shoulder.

I'd never thought of myself as uptight before. A little highly strung, maybe, but not uptight.

"Highly strung!" Jake clapped his hands together once. "You're highly strung."

"Did you just read my mind?" I muttered. "Maybe I am, but we're not kids. We're not old, sure, but Dom is almost thirty and can't keep hold of his damn keys to save his life. I just don't understand how I can be the benchmark he holds all other women to."

Jake shook his head. "You three are made for each other, I swear. Maybe he has feelings for you, Chloe. There's something there if you're the one he compares everyone else to."

"So? Why did he never tell me?"

"You never told him," Mellie pointed out.

"No, but we had a fight a few weeks ago at Peyton's, and I told him I used to have a crush on him."

"Generally, guys don't just blurt out how they feel mid-argument. There's enough emotion happening already, and we can only take so much in small doses." Jake crossed his arms. "We'll wait until a quieter time."

"Mid-argument isn't a quieter time," I said. "Especially not when he's fighting with me."

"True story," Mellie muttered.

I shot her a dark look.

Jake sighed. "All I'm saying is that I get where he's coming from. And I can't say anything else without incriminating myself."

"Do you know something I don't?" Mellie stared at him.

He shook his head. "No. Just from a guy's perspective, that's all. In the meantime, I have work to do, so while you're slacking off to be a good friend, I'll go call Peyton and order you all pizza."

"You're so sweet." Mellie smiled.

"And adjust the schedule because you'll now owe me three hours." He grinned and darted out of the office just as Mellie threw a pen and missed.

"Never date your boss," she said, looking at me.

"Or your co-boss?" I replied in a weary tone. "Because I think I have an issue with him."

Her pale-pink lips thinned into a sympathetic line. "I know, honey. I know."

***

I only knew one thing.

My head felt as though a sumo wrestler was sitting on it.

I groaned, rolling over. Coincidentally, my stomach rolled, too. I stilled, closing my eyes in the hope the room no longer spinning would help ease my nausea.

That was the last time I was going to allow Jake to make me sangria.

In fact, I don't think I ever wanted to drink sangria again.

"Here," Peyton's croaky voice made me open my eyes.

Slowly, I looked up at her. I was in her spare room, clothed except for my pants, and she was leaning over me with a glass of water and two pills.

I gingerly brought myself up to sit and leaned against the headboard. Taking the pills and glass from her, I murmured a rough, "Thank you," and took them. "How are you walking?" I asked.

"I got up an hour ago to throw up, so I didn't really have a choice," she said warily, sitting on the edge of the bed. "What the hell did Jake put in that sangria?"

I shook my head, then winced. Nope. I couldn't do that. "How much of it did we drink?"

"Too much. That's what happens when your drinking game is watching *Gordon Ramsay's Kitchen Nightmares* and taking a drink every time someone swears."

"We shouldn't do that again."

"I completely agree." She yawned and crawled across the bed, tucking herself under the covers on the other side.

"I'm not wearing pants," I told her.

She shrugged. "My shorts barely count. I'm too hungover to grope you, don't worry."

I laughed a little, then stopped quickly. Nope. Couldn't laugh, either. "Where's Mellie?" I asked.

"According to the text I woke up to from Jake, he put us both to bed, then took her home where she passed out on the sofa."

I touched my fingers to my lips. "Did he take off my pants?"

She shook her head. "I asked the same. Apparently, I yelled at him for watching me take off my pants when all he was trying to do was make sure I didn't crack my head open on the nightstand." She paused. "Then, apparently, you thought it was a good idea to take yours off, too, but you were already in bed when he checked on you."

"Oh, God," I moaned. "How embarrassing."

She shrugged a shoulder. "In your defense, you had a rough day. We were just along for the ride."

"Being kissed by the guy you've loved forever is a rough day?"

"It wasn't exactly under the moonlight though, was it? It was after a fight. That's not the romantic declaration of a fairytale forever you doodled all over your books in high school."

I sniffed. "I didn't doodle. You were the doodler."

"You were so a doodler. All I drew were cocks with faces."

"Which is why you didn't date anyone longer than two weeks in high school."

Peyt grinned. "That's because I drew cocks bigger than what they had."

She was probably right.

"What are you going to do about Dom?"

I groaned and lay on my back, staring up at the ceiling. "Nothing. I'm going to do nothing. I'm too hungover to think about anything right now."

"You have to do something. He kissed you. That means something."

I rolled my head to the side and looked at her. "From the woman who had meaningless sex for ten years."

"Hey, I had sex with them. Rarely kissed them. Kissing is intimate. It's like..." She sighed, pushing her dark hair from her face. "Kissing is baring your soul to someone else. After everything you said last night, it sounds like he kissed you because it was easier than telling you that you're his bar."

"His bar?"

"Yeah. His bar. You know, we all have a bar that something has to compare to. You're apparently his, and he's too chicken shit to say the words."

I would have rolled my eyes if my head wasn't banging harder than a frat house on a Saturday night. "I think he just wanted to get me to shut up."

"Always a possibility," she acquiesced. "But not in this context. So, what are you going to do?"

"I'm going to take a nap and pretend I didn't get blind-ass drunk last night," I answered, having another sip of water before lying back down. "And you're going to be a good friend, shut up, and nap with me."

"If I wasn't also blind-ass drunk last night, I'd argue." Peyton shuffled right down beneath the sheets and yawned. "But I was, so I won't."

I patted her on the head and turned off the light on the nightstand.

I honestly didn't think I'd be able to go back to sleep, but if I had to lie here for two hours to make her shut her mouth...

Well.

She'd never know.

CHAPTER TWELVE

CHLOE

I wish I could forget about kissing Dom as easily as I forget what I walked into a room for.

IN HINDSIGHT, GETTING DRUNK TO FORGET ABOUT DOM kissing me wasn't the greatest idea I'd ever had. It'd been almost forty-eight hours since I'd seen him last, since he'd kissed me, and I was still hungover.

From what? I didn't know. I'd drank enough water that I was no longer severely dehydrated, but my head still pounded. I hadn't been this messed up over anyone, well, ever.

I'd never cared enough about anyone to feel this way.

My stomach had tied itself into knots the second Dom's lips touched mine, and it was still that way. A tight ball of confusion and frustration that fed nausea.

I downed the rest of my coffee and leaned back against the counter, staring out of the window on the other side of the kitchen. A blur flashed as a bird flew past, and I sighed.

I was supposed to go to work today, but I didn't know how I could. I wanted to crawl back into bed and go all moody teenage girl while I tried to make sense of what was happening in my life.

Was my period coming? Was this why I was so miserable?

I needed to go to the store and stock up on donuts and candy and ice cream if that was the case.

If it wasn't... it was going to be a damn miserable week.

I pulled down the hem of my oversized t-shirt as I moved from my kitchen through to the living room. My laptop was open but asleep on the sofa, so as I sat down, I tapped the keyboard to wake it up.

It whirred to life as I looked up at the silent re-run of *Friends* that was playing on the TV. Ross kissed

Rachel in the doorway of Central Perk, and I groaned, rolling my head to the side.

Was there any escape from the kissing? Would I ever be able to escape this hell?

God, what was wrong with me? Why didn't I just confront Dom about this? God only knew I confronted him about just about everything else. This was no different to him losing his keys or putting the empty milk carton back in the fridge. It was an issue he'd caused that needed to be fixed.

But it wasn't. It was only an issue because I was in love with him and, apparently, contrary to my years-long belief, he felt something for me, too.

It was like watching a baby pick up food for the first time and wondering what the hell you were supposed to do with it.

That was what it was.

I was baby, and Dom was a carrot, and I didn't know what the hell to do.

I knew we had to talk about it. I wasn't that stupid—I was shaken up. I was confused. I was spaced out, and more than anything I really needed to get my shit together.

At least I'd showered today. That was one step toward the adulting I clearly needed to do.

Which was why I swung my feet up onto the coffee table, put the laptop on my legs, and ignored all of that. I checked and responded to emails. I sent emails to clients who'd already been on dates and agreed with one of them that the original guy wasn't quite right for her.

Adding her to my to-do list, I made a note to double-check her application, because I was pretty sure that the guy I'd matched her with had been just about perfect.

Of course, that wasn't the be all and end all of it. Someone could be perfect on paper but so, so wrong in real life.

Like me and Dom. On paper, the grand total of reasons for us to be together was a big fat zero. In reality?

Reality didn't make sense. I'd never really understood why I felt the way I did about him—I just felt it. It was the same as liking tacos or pizza.

It just was.

Love. It made no sense.

I pulled my attention from the laptop to the TV once again. I didn't know what it said about me that I had the ability to tell exactly what episode I was watching of Friends with only a few seconds of it being on, but I watched as—still on mute—Rachel cried by the window.

I felt her.

I so felt her.

I dropped my head onto the back cushions of the sofa and sighed. For a matchmaker, I had a freaking miserable love life.

The ding of my doorbell echoed through the silence of my house, and I pushed my laptop onto the cushion next to me to get up.

And stopped right before I opened the door.

I was only wearing a t-shirt. An oversized bed shirt that had a cartoon unicorn on the front... and no bra beneath it.

Thank God I had panties on.

The doorbell rang again, and I winced. "Who is it?" I shouted.

"Dom."

"Oh, shit," I whispered.

Well, there was no way he was coming in. Not when I was dressed like this. I couldn't care less about the unicorn shirt thing, but I wasn't going to open the door to him when I wasn't wearing a bra.

"I'm not here!"

"Chloe." His voice was muffled. "I can see you through the glass. And hear you."

"You can't come in!"

"Why not?"

I looked around frantically, flapping my hands. "Because I—I'm naked!"

There was a short silence and then, "I've probably seen worse."

"Ugh! I'm not really naked, but I'm not dressed for company."

Another pause. "Are you wearing those unicorn pajamas? That stupid long shirt thing?"

"Oh my God, how see-through is my glass?" I snapped, turning the key and yanking open the door.

Dom stood there, hands gripping either side of my doorframe. His gaze roved over my body, lingering for a hot second on my chest. "Not nearly as see-through as the unicorn is," he said, almost appreciatively.

I covered my chest with my arms. "What are you doing here? And how did you know I was wearing this?"

"Chlo, that thing is about fifteen years old. I'm surprised it's still held together by its stitches."

I wasn't going to tell him I'd had my mom redo the hem twice in the last five years.

"Whatever. Why are you here?"

He quirked one dark eyebrow. Disbelief shone in his eyes. "You don't know?"

"Look, if you're here to be a dick, don't bother. I'm not in the mood for it."

"I'm not." His tone was a lot more serious than a second ago. "I'm not here to be a dick, Chlo. I'm here to talk to you."

I didn't have to be Albert Einstein to know what this was about. Although, if I were, I wouldn't be in this situation in the first place, would I?

I'd be too fucking smart for this shit.

"Fine. Come in, but I need to get changed."

"Don't get changed on my account."

"I'm getting changed." I made sure my tone was more assertive, then left him standing in the doorway as I turned and stalked toward my room.

There was no way I was having this conversation in my fifteen-year-old pajamas.

Especially since, yes, this was see-through over my boobs.

***

I walked back into the kitchen.

Sans unicorn. Plus bra. Plus clean panties.

Sans visible nipples.

I was winning so far.

"All right," I said, putting my hands on my hips. "You're here to talk. Let's talk."

"Do you have any food?" Dom said, head inside my fridge. "I skipped lunch."

"It's past lunch?"

"It's two-thirty. What have you been doing all day in your teenage pajamas?"

I folded my arms over my chest. "Googling the most efficient ways to murder someone and watching Forensic Files on Netflix."

"Find anything good?" he asked, pulling open my fruit drawer. "Why is there bacon in your fruit drawer?"

"Bacon is fruit."

"Bacon couldn't be further from fruit."

"They have the same nutritional value in my eyes. God, next time you'll tell me that wine isn't really grape juice."

"It's not pure grape juice," he said, shutting the drawer.

"Watch your filthy mouth."

Dom snorted. "If you think that's filthy, you should hear me during football."

"Since when did you play football?"

"I don't," he said, closing the fridge. "But I watch it, and I'm a better coach than this city's damn team has right now," he finished on a grumble.

"Great. A couch coach. Just what the world needs more of." I sighed, passing him to the fridge. I pulled out the carton of orange juice and grabbed a glass. "Can you cut to the chase? I was working before you interrupted me."

"You were watching Friends."

"On mute. It doesn't count if it was on mute." I put the juice back in the fridge and cradled the glass in front of me. "And yes, I do know why you're here. No, I don't have the patience for this bullshit small-talk, so you have two choices."

"Do I, now?"

"Yes. You explain why you kissed me, or you fuck off."

Apparently, I could be confrontational about this. There was the Chloe I knew and loved. She was in there somewhere, just waiting to be pissed off by Dominic Austin.

Dom's lips twitched to the side, and he perched on my dining table. He crossed his arms over his chest and met my eyes, but I was momentarily distracted by the way his biceps pushed against the light gray material of his shirt.

"You're awfully confrontational for someone gaping at my arms like they've never seen a tensed bicep before." He grinned.

"You're awfully ballsy for someone who kissed me and keeps blowing me off like I'm a leaf and he's a tornado."

"I might well be a tornado for all you know."

"If you're a tornado, I'm Mother Nature, and I'm about to put your ass out." I nodded toward the knives in the holder behind me. "Talk. Now."

Dom held up both his hands. "All right, all right. Calm down, Chlo."

I glared at him.

He pushed off the table, standing up straight, and stuffed his hands into his pockets. "I don't know what I'm supposed to tell you. I don't know what you want me to tell you."

I slid my hands around my body, hugging myself. "I want to know why you kissed me. That's it. I don't want a fucking fairytale, I just want to know why."

"I wanted to." He stopped, meeting my eyes. His gaze was raw and honest, and there was no way he was lying to me.

I knew him too well.

His left cheek didn't twitch the way it had when he was sixteen and swore he hadn't sneaked out for a field party. It didn't twitch the way it had when his dad had found a condom wrapper in his pants pocket when he was seventeen, and he lied about losing his virginity.

It didn't twitch.

Not for a second.

"You wanted to?" I asked quietly. "Why? How? That doesn't make sense?"

"I know that. Shit, Chlo. You think I don't know that? I do." He scrubbed one hand through his dark hair. "I know it doesn't make sense that I wanted to kiss you. Makes even less sense that I did. All I know is that I did it and I don't regret it, so if you think I'm here to apologize, think again."

I dropped my gaze to the floor for a second. "If you apologized, you'd have a knife through your thigh right now."

"And I bet you know where that fucking artery is, don't you?"

I nodded. Once.

God bless the Investigation Discovery channel.

"Look." He took a step toward me, holding his hand out for a second before he put it back in his pocket, looking more like an awkward teen boy than a man who was thirty within a matter of months. "I get it, okay? You and I, we fight like cat and dog. I can't believe we haven't killed each other, but you can't tell me you didn't feel something the other night. You can't stand there and tell me you didn't want me the way I wanted you."

I swallowed. I didn't want to admit it. I was, shit.

I was afraid.

"It's fine. You don't have to agree, because I know you did, Chlo. You wouldn't have kissed me back if you didn't want me, too."

"Why are you here now?" My voice was scratchier than I'd wanted, but I couldn't stop my throat from being dry. It was a desolate damn desert back there.

"Because you got blind drunk last night and you're working from home today, so I know you're avoiding me."

"Someone thinks highly of himself." I snorted and pushed off the counter to walk into the front room.

His footsteps echoed after me. "You gonna deny it, Chlo? Gonna run away and tell me you didn't fucking want me, too?"

"I didn't say that!" I turned on the balls of my feet and pointed my finger at him. "I didn't say that. I'm not saying that. I'm saying fuck you, Dom. So what if I got drunk last night and spent today in my pajamas? Does it matter? That doesn't mean I'm avoiding you. That means I'm hiding while I mend my fragile, alcohol-broken consciousness."

"You're argumentative for a hungover person."

"I'm not hungover!"

"Then stop using yesterday's hangover as an excuse! I speak to my sister, you know. She told me you wolfed down a twelve-inch pizza for lunch like you'd never had anything to drink."

I was going to kill Peyton.

I threw my arm in the air. "You know what? Go. I don't want to speak to you right now. I don't want you in my house. Get lost."

"You're not walking away from me, Chloe."

I stopped and looked over my shoulder. "Looks like I am, smartass!"

He stormed toward me, grabbed my wrist, and yanked me against him. My heart thundered against my ribs, but I set my jaw and stared up at him.

"You don't get to manhandle me like I'm a wonky pancake!" I snapped, wrenching my wrist out of his grip. "Be a civilized fucking human being, goddamn it."

"You won't listen to me!" His jaw twitched.

"You aren't talking, Dominic."

He ran his hand through his hair, exasperated. "I don't know how to talk to you! You argue and fight and—fuck me, Chlo. You're impossible. I want to talk to you, but I don't fucking know how, and it's driving me insane."

I stepped back. "So, don't. Don't talk to me. Fight me. Scream at me. I don't care, just spit it out."

His nostrils flared. His inhale was deep and heavy, and his eyes shone with emotion I wasn't ready to decipher.

He rolled his shoulders, clenching his fists at his sides. His gaze flickered away from me. Dark brown eyes hit the wall next to me before they slammed into me and held my own gaze hostage.

"I want you."

I swallowed.

"I want you," he repeated. "Is that clear enough for you? Will that make you listen? Is this the fight you want? Where I stand here and tell you I didn't kiss you to shut you the fuck up? That I kissed you because I couldn't take not kissing anymore? Is that the fucking fight you want? The one where I win because I'm being so goddamn honest with you that you can't do anything but stare at me like I just stepped on your kitten?"

Yes.

Yes.

It was the fight I wanted.

And it was the fight I was going to have.

"Why then?" I asked, my voice quietly but deathly. "Was it a spur of the moment? Did you plan it? Did you actually want to do it, or was it because you had the urge?"

"I kissed you because I wanted you so damn bad it hurt. I don't need a reason for that." His eyes were on fire—a roaring furnace of anger and honesty that burned brightly. "Why did you kiss me back?"

"I don't need a reason for that!"

"You can't throw my words back at me."

"I can do whatever the hell I want!" I wanted to lash out, to hit the wall, to kick something. The anger and frustration that burned through my veins had been building for years.

I'd wanted this conversation for as long as I could remember.

Looked like I was finally getting it.

CHAPTER THIRTEEN

CHLOE

Hindsight really was a bitch.
But it had nothing on the here and now.

"YOU DON'T GET TO COME INTO MY HOUSE, INTO MY space, and demand that I be nice to you." I jabbed my finger at him. "You come in here and you be fucking nice to me, damn it."

"You wanted me to be honest, so I'm being fucking honest."

His eyes.

They were so bright.

So alive.

"Good for you. Have a gold star. My God, Dom, this isn't how it works. We've hated each other for years. You want me to suddenly accept that you want me?"

"Hated each other my left ball!" he yelled. "Fuck me, Chloe, do you believe that? Do you believe that I hate you? That I hate the person who's been my sister's best friend since she was five? That I hate the person I've seen almost every day since then? Do you really fucking think I hate you?"

"You act like it."

"And you act like you hate me, but I don't believe you." He stepped toward me. "If you hated me, you'd have kicked me out by now. You wouldn't even be thinking about listening to me. Trust me—you don't listen to me any other time, so the only reason you are right now is because you want to."

"No." I stared at him. "I'm listening to you because you keep saying you want me, but I'm wondering when you're going to prove it."

He stilled, tilting his head a little. "What?"

I threw my arms out, my stomach twisting into knots. "You're standing in front of me telling me how you want me, yet that's all you're doing. And you wonder why I don't believe you?"

"What are you saying?"

"Kiss me, idiot!"

Dom's lips parted, and his brows drew together into a frown. "What?"

"I can't make it much simpler. If you want me as much as you say you do, then kiss me, you goddamn idiot!"

Time stood still as he stayed where he was, staring at me. My skin prickled in anticipation.

Was he all talk?

Would he do it?

I knew I'd let him. Even if it never happened again, I needed the validation of a second kiss. To make sure I wasn't glorifying how amazing it was the first time around.

To make sure that my memory of the first one was real and not something I'd accidentally cooked up when I should have been working.

"Well?" I asked, raising my eyebrows. "Are you gonna? Either kiss me or get the hell out of my house."

He stalked toward me, expression unreadable, muscles visibly tensed. The veins in his forearms stood out, snaking down the insides of his arms, and one fist was clenched tight if the whiteness of his knuckles was anything to go by.

"Fine. Don't. Then you can leave. I'm not going to stand here and be confused by you. If I want to be confused, I'll reminisce about high school!" I snapped.

"I'm not hesitating because I don't want to," he said through gritted teeth. "I'm hesitating because I want you so much that if I kiss you, I don't know if I'll be able to stop."

"Did I say I wanted you to?"

"Don't fuck with me right now, Chlo."

"Then get the hell out, because you're fucking with me. Either kiss me or don't. But if you walk out now and don't kiss me, you'll never get another chance; I promise you that."

As if those words flicked a switch inside him, he reached out, clenched fist slowly moving toward my face. His hand unfurled, the backs of his fingers stroking lightly across my cheek. His eyes followed the slow movement of his hand, and only when the tips of his fingers ghosted along the curve of my jaw, making me shiver, did he lift his gaze to meet mine once again.

This wasn't heated.

This look, this connection, didn't feel as though we'd just been screaming at each other. It felt real, like there really was something hiding beneath the anger and frustration we exercised on a daily basis.

This wasn't how I'd ever planned it to be, but I couldn't look away. I couldn't clear the lump in my throat or stop the goosebumps that tickled across my skin as I waited.

For what?

For anything.

For him to move. To touch me again. To say something. To *do* something.

It felt like...

It felt like he meant it. Like this stupidly long moment where neither of us could move or speak felt like the validation I wanted.

That he wanted me.

It was the confirmation that he wasn't lying. That he meant it when he said that if he kissed me right now, he was afraid he couldn't stop. That I meant it; that I didn't want him to stop.

If that was what it took, if losing myself to him one time meant that I got to feel his lips on mine one more time, I'd do it.

I'd do it a thousand times, over and over, pressing rewind each and every single time.

I wanted to kiss him. I wanted to run my fingertips over the dark stubble that lined his jaw and chin, the very same stubble that made every curve of his lips ten times sexier than it ever had any right to be.

I wanted to close my eyes and breathe him in. Slide my fingers through his hair. Grab his t-shirt. Tear it off. Ease my hands over his body.

I wanted him.

And knowing he wanted me?

It made me do stupid things. Made me want to do stupid things.

His hand, now cupping my jaw, was hot. His fingers burned my skin, and his palm emanated warmth that I felt everywhere. I covered his hand with mine, gingerly moving to link my fingers through his.

Dom dropped his eyes to our hands for a brief second, but they met mine again when I touched my other hand to the side of his face. His stubble was short and rough, scratching against my palm in a way that was almost weirdly satisfying.

If I were a cat, I'd spend all day rubbing my palm against his jaw.

And that was the weirdest part.

"Chlo—"

I cut him off with a shake of my head. I didn't want him to speak. I wanted him to *act*. I wanted to know that he wanted me. I wanted to feel it deep down inside my bones. I wanted to know, unconditionally and irrevocably, that he wasn't here bullshitting me into next week.

So, I leaned forward, closing my eyes, and kissed him.

He didn't hesitate. His hands snaked around my body, pulling me close to him, and he kissed me back.

It was hot and heavy, deep and desperate. His tongue found mine within seconds, and I held nothing back. I wrapped my arms tight around his neck and pressed my body completely against his.

It was hard and hot, a lot like the grip he had on me. Tingles ran across my skin, causing all the hairs on my arms to stand on end, and I gasped into his mouth. I'd wanted him to kiss me, but I didn't think he'd kiss me like this.

I thought it'd be slow and tender, his lips testing mine to see how far he could go.

But this?

This was everything but. I clenched my legs together as I felt his cock harden inside his pants. It pressed against me, practically screaming out with how he wanted me.

I felt the same. My clit ached between my legs, and right now, I wished he'd let me go so I could climb him like a koala climbed a damn tree.

Dom pulled back. I peered up at him through my lashes. His eyes were dark and hooded, his jaw tight, as if he were conflicted, like he was trying to figure out how to make sense of what was happening.

"Did you mean it?" he asked, slowly bringing his eyes to mine. "If I walk out, I'll never have another chance?"

I swallowed. I did—I mean, I had meant it. But now he'd kissed me like that, did I still?

"What if I do mean it?" I asked softly. "I'm not going to sit around and wait for you to make your choice. You either want me now, or you don't want me at all."

"Chlo..." He took a deep breath, lowering his forehead to mine. "I'm not leaving. Whether you mean it or not. I don't think I can leave."

"What does that mean?"

"I'm not leaving here until I know what it's like to have you be mine."

I didn't have a chance to say anything. He dipped his face so his lips sealed over mine, rendering my words useless. All I wanted was him. His kiss, his touch, his everything.

I surrendered myself to him, completely. I didn't care. I could barely think straight, but I knew I wanted this. Whatever it took to be his for one night, I wanted it. I'd do it.

Because I wanted it, too. I wanted to be his. I wanted him to be mine. And if this was it ever was, I'd take it.

I was a fool. I knew that. There was no doubting it, no circling around it. It was sprayed on the side of my house and branded into my forehead.

But fools loved. And when they loved, they loved fully, with all the pureness in their hearts.

So, maybe there were worse things than being a fool in love.

I wound my fingers into Dom's hair. It was soft and silky and just begged to be run through my fingers.

"Be mine," Dom whispered against my lips, cupping the back of my head. "Be mine right now."

"Don't you think we'll regret this tomorrow?" I whispered.

"No, I won't. I can't regret you." He kissed me again without giving me a chance to answer.

I didn't have an answer.

I couldn't regret him either.

He pulled away once more and grabbed my hand. I followed willingly as he dragged me to the stairs and up them. He paused in the hall, looking left and right.

Grinning, I slipped past him, still holding his hand, and pulled him toward my room. No sooner had I stepped through the door than he yanked me toward him, kissed me, and dove his fingers into my hair.

Together, we staggered back toward the bed, falling when my legs hit the side of the bed. I squealed as we went down, and Dom laughed against my mouth, dipping his head as he used his hands to stop himself falling entirely on top of me.

"Don't laugh at me," I murmured, meeting his eyes.

"I'm not laughing," he said in a voice just as low and soft as mine right before he dropped his lips to mine.

My arms curled around his neck, and my knees bent to wrap my legs around his waist. Our bodies couldn't have been any closer in this moment, and goosebumps dotted my skin from the base of my neck to the tips of my fingers. A shiver jolted down my spine, making me tremble beneath him.

My heart was thumping. I couldn't hear a damn thing because my pulse thundered so harshly in my ears. All I could do was feel—feel as Dom's lips made their way over my jaw to my neck. As he kissed my skin, the pure pleasure of it making me shiver once again.

One of his hands dropped to my thigh, creeping up my leg beneath the loose fabric of the old shirt I was wearing. His fingers probed my skin as he kissed my neck. I never wanted him to stop, but my own hands had other ideas.

I grasped at the top of his t-shirt, yanking the fabric up so he could pull it over his head. He pushed up, kneeling on the edge of the bed, and tugged it over his head. I was no stranger to the sight of Dominic Austin without a shirt on, but this time, it was different.

This time, I didn't just have to look at the tight packs of muscle on his stomach or the taut muscles on his upper arms. I could touch him—I could grab his arms and run my fingers over his stomach.

Which was what I did. I trailed my fingers over his shoulders, then his chest, then his stomach. My touch faded away the closer I got to his waistband, and he shuddered as I got close to the light 'v' that dipped beneath his jeans.

Snatching my wrists up, he pressed them to the bed above my head. He dropped down, kissing me again, his hot body hovering over mine. Red-hot bolts of lust pumped through my body as his mouth danced across my skin, exploring the curve of my neck with his lips.

His hands worked my old shirt up my body higher and higher until it was bunched under my arms. I lifted my shoulders, so he could pull it over and remove it. He tossed it to the side, immediately returning his attention back to me. I was naked except for my panties, and he took full advantage of that.

His hands explored my body, from my hips to my breasts and back down again. His tongue traced a similar path, toying with the curve of my collarbone until he made his way over my chest to my nipple. I gasped as his mouth covered it and his tongue flicked.

A shiver rocketed down my spine, and I squirmed beneath him. My clit ached, and goddamn it, I'd waited too long for this. I didn't want to wait any longer. I wanted him to get up and get on with it before I went stir crazy with need.

He moved farther and farther down my body until his head was right between my legs. He dropped kisses to my lower stomach and the inside of my thighs. Tingles covered my skin as his hot mouth slid over my hip, coming closer and closer to the waistband of my last remaining piece of clothing.

Down.

He pulled down my panties, fingers hooked in the waistband. He lifted my legs as he removed them and tossed them to the side. I wriggled as his hands stroked the insides of my legs, parting them.

Kisses to the side of my thighs really had me wriggling. My heart was going crazy, and goddamn it, I could barely breathe as he moved closer and closer to my clit.

Then, he was there. Licking and sucking and toying with it. His hands clamped around my legs, holding me down, holding my hips in place against him as his tongue brought me closer and closer to the edge.

I came with a cry, and Dom's fingers dug into my thigh as he drew it out for as long as possible. My hips writhed beneath his touch, but he didn't let up until I'd stilled beneath him.

I threw my arm over my eyes when he moved. I could barely control my breathing as he moved away from me. My whole body was on fire, completely alive, and the next thing I knew, his hands were on my legs again, and he was leaning over me, kissing me.

I wrapped my arm around his neck, kissing him back. His other arm was between our bodies, and I arched my hips up, so he could move inside me.

He did, slow and easy, inch by inch, until he was fully inside. A tiny gasp escaped against his lips, and he smiled, dragging his teeth over my lower lip.

Slowly, he moved, thrusting in and out until I wrapped my legs around his body. As if he took that as his queue, he picked up the pace, moving in and out of me faster.

My nails dug into his skin as heat washed through my body once again. I was borderline delirious— pleasure pumped through my veins as we kissed, and he moved, and I grabbed at his skin. Over and over, I moaned into his mouth. He groaned a few times, too, and all that sound did was send shivers over my skin.

It felt so good. Too good. Too overwhelming and insane and unreal. I arched my back, and Dom pressed his face into my neck, kissing me.

I gripped and gripped and gripped, and then—it happened.

The orgasm washed through me like a bomb exploding. I might have screamed his name. I wasn't sure. I was barely coherent as it hit. I couldn't think or breathe or speak, or maybe I could, because who the hell knew what I could or couldn't do?

Not me.

I came back down to Earth, Dom still inside me, unmoving. His breath was hot as it fluttered against my skin with his labored exhales. His hand gently trailed up and down my side, an easy touch that felt oh-so-good.

Still, the post-orgasmic haze, I had one question.

What did we do now?

CHAPTER FOURTEEN

DOM

Emotions.
The greatest enigma of the twenty-first century.
We'd been to the moon, but we still couldn't control our
emotions.
No wonder robots were taking over.

I RUBBED MY HANDS DOWN MY FACE. MY COCK STILL throbbed with the lingering sensation of being inside her. I had no idea how long I'd been here in the bathroom, sitting on the fucking toilet trying to get my shit together.

What we'd done had changed everything. There was no chance in fucking hell that I was letting her go now. I didn't give a shit that she still owed what's-his-face a second date.

I'd wanted her for years, and now I had her, and I wasn't going to lose her. I knew I faced one hell of an uphill battle because Chloe Collins was anything but easy to understand, and I wasn't dumb enough to think that just because we'd had sex, that meant something would happen.

She'd once admitted that she'd once crushed on me.

I had a sneaking feeling that the crush wasn't as far in the past as she'd led me to believe.

I fucking hoped it wasn't.

I rubbed my hand down my face and stood up from the toilet. My left leg was goddamn dead, and I'd be limping like an idiot pretty soon when the pins and needles kicked in.

I washed my hands, using the bright, polka-dot towel on the rack to dry them, and headed back into the bedroom. What I really wanted was a shower, but I knew Chloe's temper, and if I stayed in the bathroom much longer, she'd likely accuse me of jumping out of the bathroom window.

I was naked, but that didn't mean that trail of thought was off-limits to her.

I opened my mouth to ask her what the hell we did now, but the words died on my tongue. She was wrapped around the quilt, blonde hair fanning over the pillows…

Fast asleep.

Either she hadn't slept last night, or I was better in bed than I thought I was.

And I knew I was damn good, so that was saying something.

I rubbed my hand over my jaw, then grabbed my boxers. There was no use in me trying to wake her up—I'd done that once before, and I'd almost lost my left ball, so I wasn't going to do that again anytime soon.

I finished getting dressed and headed downstairs. It was completely quiet, meaning the coffee machine seemed stupidly loud as it started up. As the hot liquid sputtered into my cup, I gripped the edge of the countertop and sighed heavily.

Of all the times for Chloe to fall asleep, it was when we needed to talk.

Then again—what the fuck did I plan to say to her anyway? There was no way that what I wanted to say to her would result in anything but an argument. That might have been our M.O., but I preferred to argue before sex rather than after it.

There was a serious lack of make-up options for post-sex arguing.

No. I wanted to tell her that she was fucking mine. That she had no business going on a date with Warren. That there were no two ways about it. I was in fucking love with her, and now that I knew there was a chance she didn't completely and utterly hate me, I wasn't going to let her go easily.

But, if I did, she'd laugh at me. She'd laugh and tell me to get the fuck out of here, because she belonged to nobody but herself, no matter what I thought.

No. If there was a chance for me and her, she had to be the one who raised the green flag. I could only push so far, but for the most part, I would wait.

God only knew I'd waited long enough for her. I could go a little longer.

I pulled my coffee mug from under the machine and finished making it. There was still no movement from upstairs, so I knew she was completely dead to the world.

Which left me with a big-ass problem.

I had a shit ton of work to do, and I didn't have my laptop with me. If I left, there was every chance she would wake up and be pissed that I wasn't there.

The last thing I wanted was for her to think I'd fucked her and then ran.

I might have done it in the past, but I'd never do it to her.

Damn it. I was fucked. And not in the way I had been thirty minutes ago.

I much preferred that one.

All right. I could leave her a note. "Gone to the office. Be right back."

Fuck though, that was lame.

I could text her. But what if she didn't see it? I didn't know where her phone was, and knowing Chloe, she'd search the whole house and yell at thin air before she ever considered finding her phone.

I was sure her soul was made of fireworks just waiting to be ignited.

My phone was still in the pocket of my jeans, so I pulled it out and opened my text message chain with my sister.

Did I really want to get her involved in this?

I didn't have a choice. I knew Chloe would tell her. There wasn't a damn thing those two hadn't told each other since the day they met—Mellie, too.

I closed that thread and opened the one with Elliott. He knew I was coming here this morning, and I also knew he wouldn't tell Peyton unless she forcibly made him.

And considering she didn't know I was here, that bought me a little time.

Me: I have a problem

As if he'd been waiting, his response came quickly.

Elliott: You fucked her, didn't you?
Me: Yes.
Elliott: You know I'm going to have to delete this whole conversation, so I'm gonna need to know when we're done talking.

And there was how he'd keep it from Peyton.

Me: She's asleep. Fell asleep before we could talk. I need to work, but I can't leave.
Elliott: Write a note?
Me: Would you leave Peyton a note?
Elliott: Not if I wanted to keep my balls. Point taken. Can you use her laptop?

Why the fuck didn't I think of that?

I grabbed my coffee and walked into the living room. A quick glance around showed it open on the sofa cushion, and a look toward the TV made me groan.

Friends. How many fucking times could one person watch one show and not get sick of it?

I set my cup on the coffee table and woke up the laptop. A sign-in screen blinked at me, asking me for the password.

Fuck. Of course, it had a password. It was Chloe. She'd password her front door if she could.

God only knew she'd password mine. I couldn't lose the keys then.

Elliott: Any luck?

Me: Needs a password. What would it be?

Elliott: Something obvious. Peyton's are mostly either her middle name and date of birth or her favorite things.

Me: I'm hacking her email and marking all the spam as not spam.

Elliott: Definitely deleting this conversation.

He was smarter than I was.

I sighed and typed in her middle name followed by her date of birth.

Nope. Not that combination.

I tried a few more, including just her middle name, adding caps, adding symbols—nothing. I was on the verge of giving up when a little message asking me if I wanted a hint popped up.

Fucking yes. I did want a hint.

"Work Date."

I frowned. What the hell did that mean? I'm sure it was a hint for her, but...

Work.

Stupid Cupid.

Was the business really her password?

I typed it in and hit enter. Still wrong, but that was the only work it could—

Shit. I knew what that meant.

I re-typed the name and added her date of birth. A little circle came up that it was loading, and I held my breath until the screen blinked to the desktop.

Thank God for that.

I really needed to talk to her about password security...

Me: Got in. Figured out the password hint.

Elliott: Good to know. What are you gonna do now?

The only thing I could do.

Me: Wait for her.

***

"Sorry, Tanya," I said quietly into the phone. "We've been working together now for nine months. I can't help you if you're going to reject every guy I send your way on the first date."

"I know. You're right. I'm sorry. I just think I'm not ready to commit," she replied.

"Why don't I send you my sister's way? She'll be able to help you out," I offered.

A moment's silence, and then, "That sounds like it might be better right now. Thanks, Dom."

"You're welcome. Speak soon." I hung up and pinched the bridge of my nose.

I wasn't gonna lie. She was one of the most high-maintenance clients I'd ever worked with. Fifteen dates in nine months and every single one of them was wrong. After she'd slept with the last three on the first date only to never speak to them again, it was pretty obvious she was more designed for Peyton's hook-up services than she was my dating ones.

I blew out a long breath and leaned my head back on the sofa. Closing my eyes, I let the frustration of my wasted time escape me. I stayed like that for a moment, then pushed the laptop off me, grabbed my empty coffee mug, and got up to make another.

I walked into the kitchen and stopped. Chloe was standing in front of the machine, wearing the same, oversized shirt she'd had on when I'd gotten here. This time, though, she was clearly wearing a bra and a pair of neon yellow shorts beneath it.

She dropped her hands to the hem, tying the side of the shirt into a knot. Slowly, she tilted her head so her eyes found mine.

"You're awake," I said like an idiot.

"And you're still here," she said gently.

I put down my cup next to the machine and looked down at her. "Why wouldn't I be?"

"Well, I fell asleep, for a start." She tucked some of her messy hair behind her ear. "I didn't expect you to be here when I woke up. I thought you'd have gone to work."

"I did. I used your laptop and turned off that shit you were watching on TV."

Her eyebrows shot up. "I don't know what to address first. The blasphemy or the fact you broke into my laptop."

"It's not breaking in when you have an obvious password hint." I nudged her to the side and put my cup under the machine. ""Work Date." Stupid Cupid, plus the date we were officially registered as a company, which happened to be on your birthday."

"Great. Now I have to change my password."

"Why? I don't need it from now on."

She pointed to the Echo on the other side of the room.

My lips quirked up. "I can say, in good faith, that one of the richest men in the world is not interested in your laptop password, Chlo."

She folded her arms. "But people still listen through it."

"Then why do you keep it?"

"Because," she said, shooting it a glance. "There was this murder case where the judge ordered them to hand over mic footage, and it totally pinned the murderer."

"So, you're keeping it on the off chance you get murdered, and they don't leave enough evidence behind?"

She nodded. "You never know." Then, she swiped my now-full mug from the machine. "Thanks for the coffee."

"That was mine."

"I know, but I just woke up, and the don't-talk-until-coffee rule applies to all kinds of sleep. All night or catnap—I'm not fussy." She pulled the milk from the fridge.

"I've been drinking from it."

"Oh, God, alert the germ police. God forbid I drink from the mug of a man who had his tongue on my clitoris a few hours ago."

That was a very solid point.

"I see we're not beating around the bush when it comes to discussing it."

She slammed down the carton of milk and looked at me. "What? Are we not supposed to? Are we just going to ignore it happened?"

This was escalating faster than I'd imagined.

"Also, I don't have a bush to beat around, as you well know." She poured the milk into the coffee and replaced it.

Thank God.

The next step was to get out of the kitchen. If she was yelling already, then this was a dangerous room.

Never mind the little computer thing recording her murder. It'd record mine if we stayed in here much longer.

"All fair points you're making." I nodded, getting another mug. "But, I'd rather not have this conversation in the kitchen. You can reach the knives too easily."

"I've already told you, I'm not going to kill you. Not until we get life insurance policies." She grinned over the rim of her mug and walked into the living room.

I shook my head slowly. Two minutes ago, she was yelling at me; now she was grinning. What the fuck was in her coffee? Did she drug herself on the sly? No random bean was that magic. This wasn't Jack and the fucking Beanstalk.

I finished making my coffee and joined her in the living room. She'd wasted no time putting her stupid show back on again, and I bit back a sigh as I took my seat on the sofa.

"So," she said, blowing on her coffee with her eyes trained on the TV. "What do we do now?"

"We can do it again if you really want. I won't object."

"Dom. I'm being serious." Chloe rested the mug on the arm of the chair and turned to look at me. Vulnerability flashed in her eyes, and it was clear that the niggling feeling I'd had was right.

I wasn't the only one feeling something they shouldn't be feeling.

She swallowed, looking down at her legs. She picked a piece of thread off her leg, twisting it around her finger until it snapped when she dropped it on the floor.

"It's not a joke. I know that, Chlo," I said quietly, keeping my eyes on her. "It's not even close to being funny."

"Why did you do it?" She lifted her gaze. "Why did you kiss me, then come here, and..." she trailed off, instead choosing to wave her arm in the direction of the stairs.

"Because I wanted to," I said. "Because I wanted you."

"Wanted?"

"You say that like I'm telling you that's changed."

"Your use of the past tense suggests it has."

I put the mug down, getting up and walking over to her. I sat on the edge of the coffee table, leaning forward with my elbows on my knees, and looked right at her. "It doesn't change anything. I still want you as much as I did when I walked in that door a few hours ago."

She didn't say anything. She simply looked back down at her legs.

"Whether or not I want you isn't the question. The question is do you want me?"

She glanced up, lips parted before she looked back down.

"Chloe..."

She nodded. That was it—her answer. Three little jerks of her head where she couldn't even look at me.

"Then—"

"Argh!" Chloe stood up, diving her fingers into her hair. She fisted the already messy curls, tugging at them as she turned her back to me.

That wasn't the reaction I was expecting.

"You can't expect this would work." She turned, piercing me with her bright eyes. "Me and you. The idea is just... insane."

My eyebrows shot up. "You didn't think it was so insane when you told me that I'd never have another chance with you if I left."

"I didn't think you'd stay," she admitted. "I wanted you to, but I didn't think you would."

"You can't think I would have left."

"You'd kissed me two days before. I didn't know what to think. I still don't." She ran her fingers back through her hair again and turned to face me. "We fight all the time, Dom. That doesn't make for a successful anything, and I'm not going to be your fuck buddy."

I got up and walked over to her. "Peyton and Elliott fight all the time. So do Mellie and Jake. Besides, it's more bickering."

"Three weeks ago, I threw a water bottle at you."

"Eh. I deserved it. I had actually eaten your last Sour Patch Kids."

Her jaw dropped. "So, you lied to me?"

I held up my hands. "Hey. You threw it at me when you thought it was Peyton. Like I was gonna tell you it was really me."

"Oh, you—"

I grabbed her wrists before she could hit me. "It doesn't matter that we fight. I don't fucking care."

"Well, I do. I want to be with the cream to my strawberries, not the oil to my water."

"Oh, please. You'd be bored out of your mind if you ever dated someone who was the cream to your strawberries. They wouldn't fight you nearly as much as you need to be fought."

"What if I found the cream to my strawberries?"

I stepped back and let go of her hands. "Then everything you've said to me today has been nothing but a big waste of time, and I have somewhere else to be." I picked my phone up from the sofa and shoved it into my pocket.

"Dom."

I stopped in the doorway and looked back at her.

"This is why," she said quietly, wrapping her arms around her waist. "This is why we would never work."

"No, Chloe. We'll never work because you're not willing to try. There's the difference. I'd go to the ends of the Earth to try. Yet, you tell me you want me, then tell me there's someone better out there for you than me." I shrugged. "Fine. I might lose my keys or do things that annoy you or fight with you, but if you think someone else is better for you, go get him. But I can bet my life savings he'll never see that the office kitchen is out of coffee and get the last pods from his own kitchen just so you can have yours. He'll never swap your tape rolls when yours is getting low just so you don't run out, even though he knows you'll get annoyed that he's run out. He'll never buy your favorite flavored water in his own grocery shop just to make sure you always have it in the fridge when you get thirsty at work."

"You do all those things?" she said softly, lips parted.

"Of course, I do. I also change out your pens when the ink is getting low and make sure your computer is connected to the WiFi after a power outage. I also make sure there's enough ink in the printer if I know you need to print stuff. I even switched our keyboards that time yours stopped working and bought a new one, then switched them back just so you had the new one." I shoved my hands in my pockets. "Just... making sure it's not hard for you to do your job. Working with me is frustrating enough without having to cope with all that."

She looked away, swallowing hard. I swore there were tears in her eyes, and that twisted my gut into fucking knots. Stupid stuff—stupid shit that had become a routine for me that I thought she knew about.

I walked over to her, instantly bringing my hands to her face. She was crying, and I hated it. I hated that I was the reason she was crying. I hated that I'd said all that when I should have just taken her at her word and left.

"Don't cry," I whispered. "God, Chlo. Don't cry."

"Why?" she whispered back, lifting her tear-filled eyes to me.

I watched as one tear spilled over and caught it with my thumb. "Because. I'm fucking crazy about you."

CHAPTER FIFTEEN

CHLOE

What. A. Clusterfuck.

DOM DIPPED HIS HEAD, TOUCHING HIS FOREHEAD TO mine. His hot breath danced across my parted lips, and his thumbs gently swiped away a tear that escaped from the corner of my eyes.

If I had to tally how many times I'd wanted to hear those words from his lips, then I was gonna need more paper.

Now, it'd happened. He'd told me the one thing I'd always wanted to hear, except now I wasn't sure I did.

Up until a few days ago, I'd made my peace that this was over. I had to move on, and we'd never be together.

Then, I'd gotten drunk.

I'd gotten drunk, and before I'd passed out, I'd texted Warren about a second date. Something I'd forgotten about until I'd woken up forty-five minutes ago and saw his text asking if we were still on for tonight.

I couldn't think of anything that I wanted to do less, especially after what had happened today. But, I couldn't cancel. It was too late, and I didn't really have a viable excuse to cancel.

"I'm seeing Warren tonight," I whispered.

Dom's inhale was sharp, as was the way he released me. I swiped at my cheeks, furiously removing the lingering wetness from the few tears that had made it past his thumbs.

I opened my mouth to explain why I was going, how it had happened—but I couldn't. Even if I did, I knew it'd be a waste of time.

Because he didn't give me the chance to explain.

By the time I'd formed a sentence in my brain, my front door slammed shut.

I slid over to the chair and crumpled into it. No more tears came out, but I stared through the little view I had to the hall and at the front door. I wanted him to turn around and come back and demand to know why, but I knew he wouldn't.

That was Dom.

He was like Peyton. He'd fight you until he was blue in the face, but the second you hurt him, he was done talking to you.

And I'd hurt him. I didn't need to be a genius to figure it out. Fuck, he'd just said everything I'd ever wanted to hear, and my response was to tell him that we'd never work, and I was seeing another guy for dinner tonight.

I buried my face in my hands. What was wrong with me? He was literally everything I'd ever wanted, and I was running away from the situation like he was trying to poison me.

My phone rang from somewhere in the house. I ignored it. I didn't want to speak to anyone right now. I didn't care if it was my mom or one of my best friends or even Dom himself.

I just needed to be alone.

I needed to be alone to figure this all out in the hopes I didn't fuck everything up.

Any more than I already had, that was.

***

I put the phone face down on my bed and stared at it. I had it on silent because I was supposed to meet Warren in an hour, yet I was seriously thinking about canceling. I knew he'd be on his way, and this all made me a terrible, terrible person.

To everyone.

I wasn't sixteen, so why the hell was I acting like it? I was twenty-seven, for the love of God. I needed to get my shit together. I either wanted Dom, or I wanted to see where it went with Warren.

He was the easy choice, believe it or not. He had everything I wanted in the perfect guy.

But he wasn't Dom. And being the perfect guy didn't necessarily equal being the right guy. If Warren was the right guy, I wouldn't be thinking about canceling the second date.

Would I?

No. I knew the answer.

But did that mean Dom was the right one?

I picked up my phone and opened my group chat with Mellie and Peyton. Apparently, being alone wasn't cutting it. It'd been three hours, and all I'd achieved was folding my clean towels.

Me: I had sex with Dom.

As expected, the messages came thick and fast.

Peyton: WHAT
Mellie: REAL SEX OR DREAM SEX
Peyton: WHAT
Peyton: WHAT THE
Mellie: Chloe explain
Peyton: WHAT THE FUCK
Peyton: WHEN DID THIS HAPPEN

Peyton: HOW DID THIS HAPPEN

Mellie: I think the how is pretty obvious, Peyt

Me: He slipped on a banana peel, and his penis accidentally ended up inside my vagina.

There. That ought to explain it.

Peyton: Well, shit. Elliott's been putting it in the wrong hole the entire time.

Mellie: Well, he'll be disappointed when he moves from your asshole to your vagina.

Peyton: He's never put it in my ass.

Me: She meant your mouth.

Peyton: Please explain how you ended up having sex with my brother.

Me: Like, from the start? Because I don't have time for that. I'm in a crisis over here.

Me: We had a fight, then we had sex, then we had another fight, except in that fight he told me he wants me and is crazy about me and all the little things he does that he never told me about.

Mellie: THIS IS GREAT!!! Why are you in crisis?

Me: Remember how your boyfriend got me drunk and I texted Warren?

Mellie: Oh no (Phoebe's voice)

Me: Oh yes. He literally said, "I'm crazy about you," and idiot over here goes, "I'm seeing Warren tonight."

Mellie: You're not still seeing him, are you?????

Me: I don't know. I'm supposed to meet him in an hour, but I don't know what to do.

Mellie: You tell him something came up, an emergency, and you order pizza because I'm on my way over.

Me: You don't need to come over.

Mellie: I'm supposed to meet Jake's highly-Christian aunt tonight. I need to come over. What a shame. I'll pick you up on the way, Peyt.

Me: Well, okay, but this is me doing you a favor, you know.

Mellie: I'll stop for ice cream, too.

Me: K. We're even.

***

"Where's Peyton?"

Mellie put a brown grocery bag on the coffee table and grimaced at me. "I went there, but she said she couldn't come because Elliott was on his way over."

I blinked at her. "What? I need her, and what?"

"Oh, he was already there. He laughed and told her she was a shit-ass liar, which she is." She pulled out two cartons of Ben and Jerry's ice cream. "Dom was on his way over there. She didn't want me to tell you because she didn't want you to think she was choosing him over you."

I rolled my eyes. "She'll be texting you all night finding out what I'm saying."

"She will." She grinned, both cartons of ice cream in her hands. "And I told her to fuck off, she knows where we'll be."

A gentle laugh escaped me, and I fluffed my fingers through my hair. I'd taken a shower after texting

Warren and canceling due to a family emergency, and my hair had dried in a wavy mess—the kind that looked cute on little kids after they'd had wet braided hair.

Not so much on me.

"Okay, that's in the freezer." She put the bag on the floor and dropped onto the sofa with me. "What happened?"

I told her everything. The words flowed out of me like water from a faucet. From the second he knocked on the door until the moment he slammed it on his way out.

Mellie twisted her lips to the side, looking at me with more than a little sympathy in her eyes. "Don't take this the wrong way," she said slowly and softly. "But this is everything you've wanted. You're in love with him. Why do you feel this way?"

"Because I made peace with it." I pushed my hair from my face and rested my elbow on the back of the sofa to prop up my head. "I put every idea I had of us being together away and, for the first time, I was really serious about moving on. I was totally okay with the idea that I had to get over him, and I think I really could have done it."

"If he hadn't kissed you."

I nodded. "If he hadn't kissed me."

"Okay, but you can still do it. Just because you've kissed him and had sex with him doesn't mean you still can't move on. Or you should get a kitten and fall in love with that instead."

I paused. That wasn't really a bad idea. But kittens did need a lot of attention... "I don't know if I have the patience for a kitten."

She thought about it for a moment and said, "You're right. You definitely don't. But you still have the option to get over him. I think it's totally okay for you to say, 'I don't want to do this anymore, it's time to move on.'"

I chewed on the corner of my thumbnail. "But are there too many questions with that? I feel like if I do that, then I have to explain why I don't want to do it anymore. Plus, we work together. We co-own the business. I can't just turn that off or never see him again."

"Working together does throw a wrench in the works. Have you considered maybe finding another job?"

"More times than I can count," I muttered. "I love my job. And I love him. But is it enough to be with each other twenty-four-seven and not want to murder each other? How do you and Jake do it?"

The doorbell went just as Mellie opened her mouth to speak. She held up a finger and jumped up before I could move. Returning seconds later with a grin on her face, she put the pizza box on the cushion between us and got comfortable.

"First," she said. "I'm going to say that you and Dom want to murder each other anyway, but that's just how you work. And, honestly? It makes a hell of a lot more sense now that it's out in the open about how he feels about you. You fought because you cared about each other but had to keep all that emotion inside, almost all the time."

Damn it. She was onto something.

"Now that you have it all out in the open, you shouldn't be at each other's throats nearly half as much."

"Well, he has it out in the open. I didn't do much talking," I admitted. "And I definitely didn't tell him completely how I feel, but I think he knows I feel something."

"At least y'all are catching up to what the rest of us have known for a while." She shrugged and opened the pizza box. "You're trying to base your decision on what your relationship is like now, but it'd be totally different. And second, me and Jake work because we're not together all the time. If we work all day together, we'll eat lunch together, but spend the evenings apart. He's not there as much as he used to be, but it's all balance."

"Like how you're here tonight when you should be meeting his family."

"You should be on a date."

"I'm having a crisis."

She wiggled her slice of pizza at me. "And I'm helping with the crisis like a good best friend." A grin stretched across her face before it dropped, and she put her pizza back into the box. "Honestly, Chlo, I think Dom's right in a way about you not being willing to try. I think you're willing; I just think you've wanted to be with him for so long that you're too scared to try."

And, there it was.

She'd nailed it. She may as well have whacked me on the head with a hammer because that was the goddamn truth.

I'd wanted to be with him for years, and now the prospect was in front of me, it was terrifying.

"You're right," I said, picking a stringy bit of cheese on the pizza. "I think... I think I'm so afraid of losing him that I'd rather never have him at all."

Mellie gave me a sympathetic smile. "Exactly. But is that worth knowing you'll always have to wonder what could have happened?"

I opened my mouth to answer, then stopped.

I didn't have an answer.

I couldn't answer that.

And you know what?

I didn't want to know the answer.

CHAPTER SIXTEEN

DOM

Fuck this. Fuck it. Fuck everything.
Especially fuck that douchebag I stupidly set her up with.
And especially, especially fuck my heart.

AWKWARD SILENCE REIGNED SUPREME IN MY SISTER'S living room. Nobody talked. The TV was on, just loud enough that it wasn't the kind of awkward that made you want to get up and run away, but not so loud it was too much. The scratch of fingers against the bottom of a pizza box broke my concentration of staring into space as I blinked and focused just in enough time to catch Peyton stealing the last slice of my pizza.

She grinned, eyes sparkling, and bit down on the slice.

I shook my head. I wasn't going to fight her. I didn't have it in me. The day with Chloe had left me both mentally and physically exhausted, and knowing that she was spending the evening with Warren?

It sucked. I couldn't believe she'd said those words to me—that I'd poured my soul out to her, told her everything about how I felt, and that had been her response.

In hindsight, she hadn't said it to be spiteful. I knew that—hell, I knew it then. She'd said it just to tell me, and while her timing had left an awful lot to be desired, I hadn't given her a chance to explain how it had come around.

I hadn't given myself a chance not to ask her to go. Even if she refused and said she had to, for whatever reason, I wish like fuck I'd stopped and asked her.

Now, she was probably out with him, and it was eating me inside.

I should never have acknowledged my feelings for her. Never should have gone along with that stupid dating thing. All I'd done was lost and lost again. My date was a bust, and I may well have broken my own goddamn heart in the process.

"So," Elliott said, wiping his hands on his jeans. "What are you gonna do?"

I glanced at Peyton.

"I know you fucked her," she said around a mouthful of pizza. "She texted me. Something about a crisis."

"A crisis? Didn't sound like a damn crisis when she told me she was seeing Warren tonight."

Peyton quirked an eyebrow.

"She's going on a date with him tonight?" Elliott choked on his beer. "What?"

I shrugged a shoulder. "I didn't hang around to ask. She told me, and I just left."

"You just left?" Peyton asked.

"That's the thing you're bothered about?"

"No, but, I mean, we were drunk when she texted him. As in, Jake made sangria, and we were white-girl wasted to the point that, if we'd been out dancing, we'd have been flashing our asses as we strolled down Bourbon Street."

"What are you saying?" I narrowed my eyes at her.

"I'm not saying anything." She held up her hands, but she didn't look at me. "I'm just saying that she's probably going out with him because she feels like she has to. That doesn't mean she wants to. Haven't you ever been on a date you'd rather gauge out your eyeballs with a rusty fork than go on?"

I grimaced, nodding. "Fuck."

"I don't know, because you showed up before I could talk to her more, but that's my guess." Peyton shrugged a shoulder. "She was drunk and confused and, more than a little upset that you'd kissed her—"

"She was upset?"

Elliott did a double-take. "Upset? Why the hell was she upset?"

Peyton looked at him. "She accepted they'd never be together, then fucking Romeo over here goes and messes that up."

"Wait," I said.

She froze. "Fuck a fox."

Elliott patted her knee.

Sheepishly, Peyton turned to me and scratched the side of her neck. "Yes?"

I sat forward, shuffling on the cushion. "What do you mean by that? That she accepted we'd never be together?"

"Um. I don't know if I'm the best person to explain that."

"You're not getting out of this. What the hell do you mean by that?"

She shifted. "I don't want to play twenty questions. Can we try shots instead? Yep. Let's do shots." She got up, but Elliott grabbed hold of her arm and dragged her back down.

"No. You slipped up, so now you've got to finish what you and your big mouth started," he said, wrapping both arms around her chest and holding her down.

She licked his arm.

"Not gonna work. I'm not letting go until you tell him. And if you don't, I will."

"Oh, that's dirty!" Peyton sputtered.

"Can someone just tell me what the fuck you're talking about?" I threw my arms out. "I'm so fucking confused."

She sighed, then sat up, still held down by Elliott. "All right. Fine. I'll tell you. Remember a few weeks ago when y'all had a fight here? About you losing your keys and the tax forms?"

I nodded. "She told me she couldn't believe she once had a crush on me while you two shamelessly watched."

Elliott gave me a thumb up. "That's the one."

"Well." Peyton shifted when he loosened his grip on her. "She wasn't entirely truthful when she said she'd *had* a crush on you. It's more like she's been in love with you for a really long time."

I stared at her.

"And by a really long time, I think since we were kids."

What the fuck?

"And you never told me?" I wasn't even angry. I was numb. "You knew how I felt about her. How could you not tell me?"

"It wasn't my business, Dom. It wasn't my place to tell either of you how the other felt and the only reason I'm doing it now is because you're so damn close, and I don't think she'll tell you herself." She crossed her arms and sat back. "And, you know. I put my foot in my mouth."

I dropped back into the chair. "I don't believe this."

"I'm sorry," she said. "I wanted to tell you. Believe me, I've wanted to tell both of you everything, so you'd get on with it, but I promised myself I wouldn't unless it looked like you were doing it yourselves."

I ran my hand through my hair. I had no idea what to think about that. I couldn't believe what she'd told me. Hell, when Chloe had admitted that she'd had a crush on me, I thought she meant a crush.

As in, I was attractive, she wanted to kiss me, and she had minor feelings for me.

Not that she'd been in love with me since we were fucking children.

In love.

She was in love with me.

"Does she still feel like that now?" I asked, looking at Elliott. I knew he'd give me a straight answer. He had no loyalty to Chloe the way Peyton did.

He hesitated, and that momentary silence gave me the answer before he opened his mouth. "Yes. She does. That's why this is such a mess."

"Why does that make it a mess? She loves me. I'm in love with her. What is messy about that?"

"Everything." Peyton got up and stalked into the kitchen. The fridge opened, and there was a clink, and she returned with a bottle of half-empty wine in her hand.

"Explain," I demanded.

She sat and unscrewed the cap of the wine. "You have to understand that she hoped for ages that something would happen between you two. We're not talking six months—we're talking teens and her entire adult life so far. She couldn't get over you because you're together so much and it was impossible."

"So, about how long you've been waiting for a Hogwarts letter," I said.

"It could still happen, thank you very much." She recapped the wine and put it on a slate coaster. "About a month ago, she realized it would never happen.

Neither of you had ever shown any signs of making a move on the other, and I think she finally made peace with that. She was ready to move on, Dom. She *wanted* to. As far as she was concerned, you hated her, second only to how you tolerated her."

"Shit." I rubbed my hand down my face.

"Then… you kissed her, and you literally fucked up everything she'd come to terms with. Now, she's all kinds of confused, because everything she thought would never happen has potential to happen."

Elliott shook his head. "Women. Fucking women."

Never was a truer statement spoken.

"But… I want everything she wants," I said to Peyton. "Why is that so hard for her to accept?"

"Because! Ugh, you absolute lumphead." She smacked her hand against her forehead. "She accepted it would never happen. It was done. Finito. Never. Gonna. Happen."

"Well, if she'd told me how she felt, it would have happened."

"You could have told her. You had plenty of opportunities before you started to work together and verbally kill each other on a daily basis. It's not her fault you never noticed all the times she was mega-bitch on the jealousy scale or—"

"When the hell did that happen?"

"Well, most recently? Ruby."

I stared at her. "I thought she just hated Ruby."

"She did. She looked like a fifty-cent hooker stuffed into a five-hundred-dollar wrapper," Peyton said, matter-of-factly. "The point remains, she's spent years watching you be with other people and being jealous. Treating you differently. Dropping hints. Just being someone who's in love with you, while you've literally kept it all locked up and not even given a hint of knowledge that you were interested in her. It's not her fault you were too dense to see it."

"Wait—are you blaming me for all this?"

"Your timing was pretty bad, dude," Elliott said.

Peyton nodded. "I am. I have to blame somebody, and you're the logical target right now."

"I'm your brother. What happened to sibling loyalty?"

Hitting me with a scathing glare, she said, "Sibling loyalty went out the window the day you made all my Barbies punk rockers."

I shook my head. "I should have known that would come back to bite me."

"Hindsight is a wonderful thing, bro." She grinned and stood up. "I'll be right back."

I sighed when she left the room. "You agree with her?" I asked Elliott.

He shrugged a shoulder. "Dunno. I'm not as involved in this as she is, you know?"

"What would you do if you were me?"

"If I was in this situation with Peyton?"

"Yeah."

"I'd take out any motherfucker in the path between me and her," he said honestly, looking me dead in the eye. "You've been in love with her for, what? Ten years? And now the chance is finally here? Fuck, Dom. You can't let it go. Even if she tells you no in the end, you have to fight for her. You'll regret it if you don't."

"She doesn't think it'll work."

"Neither did Peyton and now I think she spends more time with Briony than I do." His lips twitched to one side. "She picked her up from preschool and took her to the movies last week. You just have to prove to Chloe that you're willing to do whatever it takes to convince her it'll work. No matter what it takes."

"Easier said than done," I muttered.

A happy sigh sounded from the doorway as Peyton walked back in. "What are we talking about?"

"The draft," Elliott said without batting an eyelid.

"Is a window open?" she asked.

"The football draft."

"Oh. I don't care about that. Carry on." She picked up her phone and scrolled.

"Did you talk to Chloe?" I sat up straight.

She peered over at me. "No. I had to pee. Why would I talk to her while I pee unless she's here and can bring me more toilet paper?"

I wanted to believe her, but the sparkle in her eye said she knew a lot of things I didn't.

And, unfortunately for me, I had the feeling my sister had spilled enough secrets for one night.

CHAPTER SEVENTEEN

CHLOE

Sometimes, you just have to be honest.
Maybe not so blunt, though.

I HAD A PLAN.

After too much ice cream and pizza culminating in a trip to a drive-thru cocktail place, Mellie stayed the night. We watched endless episodes of *Friends*, mostly the ones that consisted of Ross and Rachel's relationship, and formed a plan.

I was going to go to work today, pull up my big girl panties, and come clean.

Honesty, I felt like I was surrendering to the cops, and I hadn't even done anything wrong.

No. We'd come to the conclusion that the only way I could be remotely successful at moving on was if I bit the bullet and was completely honest. If I decided to move on from my feelings toward Dom, I had to clear the air and let them all out.

So. I was going to walk into the office, put my foot down, and admit to him that I was in love with him and had been for a long time.

At least, that was my plan.

Like I said. I had one. Whether or not I was coherent enough to execute it was a whole other story.

I sipped on my iced Starbucks coffee and bumped the main door open with my hip. It swung open easily, and my stomach skipped at the thought that Dom was already inside.

Luckily, the locked door to the office bought me some time. I dug my keys out of my purse and unlocked it. It was eerily silent, but I was thankful for it.

Actually, no. I wasn't. Silence meant one thing; overthinking.

How was I supposed to tell Dom the truth? After what I'd said to him last night... Jesus, I was going to look like I had a split personality. It damn well felt like it for the most part. I'd been living a lie with him for years.

Our entire relationship had changed, and I didn't know if it was for the better.

I was afraid. I was afraid that if I made the choice to try something between us, it'd go wrong. Then, I wouldn't just lose the person I'd loved forever—I'd lose my business partner and my friend.

Even if our friendship was wildly fucked up. Then again, all the best friendships were fucked up. God knew the one I shared with Peyton and Mellie was at times.

Hell.

I sat at my desk, dumping my purse on the floor and my coffee on my llama coaster. My PC screen came to life with the nudge of my mouse, and I typed my password—that Dom apparently now knew—to get into it.

I didn't know why. I wasn't in the mind to work yet, but it was weirdly comforting. Mostly because I immediately went to my Amazon and clicked to stream another episode of *Friends*.

It was like a comfort blanket, and the familiarity of the episodes and the characters helped me not freak out as I waited.

Who knew it was so hard to tell someone you were in love with them?

Granted, I expected this moment would be when I was in a relationship and happy and knew the outcome. Instead, I was torn, confused, and had no idea about what would happen when I admitted to Dom exactly how I felt about him.

Our relationship was weird. So fucking weird. It didn't make sense, and I wasn't sure it ever would, no matter what happened. And I was okay with that—at least, I was pretty sure I was.

Either way, I didn't have a choice. I had to be okay. Whether I made the choice to put this part of my life to bed or keep it alive, I had to be okay with the outcome in order to make that choice.

I sipped my coffee and watched my screen. I really needed a way out. Could I get a tunnel? Could someone smuggle me out of New Orleans?

I'd spent too much time with Peyton. I was being a regular little drama queen.

Sigh. Sigh. Sigh.

Couldn't I write a love letter? Or was that too eighteen-hundreds? Was that a thing then? Was that still a thing now? I got them in elementary school. Awkward, hand-scribbled notes stuffed into my backpack...

And to think, I thought they were bad.

Nothing compared to adulthood.

Can I take back all the times I ever wanted to be a grown-up?

No?

Well, that sucked.

The door to the offices opened, and my head jerked up in enough time to see Dom still in the doorway.

My eyes met his. Did he see in mine what I saw in his? Confusion and uncertainty? Raw emotion and worry?

A part of me hoped he did.

"Hi," I said.

"Hi. I didn't expect you to be here so early." He stepped inside and shut the door behind him.

"Oh. I'm not working," I said, right as Monica Geller screamed, "I know!" on the screen.

Dom's lips twitched to one side. "You're watching that stupid TV show."

"You're not allowed to call it that. I've never called your favorite TV shows stupid."

"I'm pretty sure you spent the entirety of high school complaining about football."

"I didn't call it stupid, though."

"Probably somewhere along the line."

"Nobody keeps track of that." I sniffed and paused the streaming. "How was your night with New Orleans' hottest couple?"

He wrinkled his face up. "How did you—never mind." He shook his head and hit me with a darker look than before. "How was your date with Baton Rouge's most eligible bachelor?" He stormed out of view before I could respond.

I swallowed back a ball of nerves that ultimately exploded in my stomach. "Dunno. You'll have to ask him. He's the only one who went," I called.

Silence.

Then, he walked backward into my office, one eyebrow quirked questioningly. "You stood him up?"

"No." I shifted. "He just happened to already be on his way when I canceled."

Dom moved, leaning against the wall. His arms tensed as he folded them across his chest. He didn't say anything—he merely looked at me, waiting.

"I was drunk when I texted him." I glanced down. "I didn't even know until I saw his text asking if we were still on for the date when I woke up yesterday."

Still, he didn't speak. Just stared at me, his dark eyes piercing my soul.

I fidgeted with a small stack of Post-it sticky notes. "Mellie came over instead. She talked me down from a lot of stuff. I think."

"What did she say?"

I let go of a heavy breath and said, "That it's still okay if I'm ready to get over you."

Dom took a deep breath, then shrugged one shoulder. "She's right. It is. If that's what you really want to do."

"I don't know." I put my foot on the edge of the chair and hugged my thigh to my chest. "See, Dom, here's the thing. I've loved you for as long as I can remember."

His jaw twitched.

"Not a silly crush that I could get over in a heartbeat as soon as the next hot guy came along. I can't remember not being in love with you, and I finally—finally—accepted that you would never feel that way about me. And you know what drove that point home?"

I was going to throw up.

He shook his head.

"You set me up with Warren." I rested my cheek on my knee. "I told myself that if you set me up with him without question, I was right. Nothing would ever happen between us, and you did it."

He ran his hand through his hair. "But I didn't—"

"It didn't matter that you didn't know. How was I supposed to tell you? You're Peyton's brother. As far as I was concerned, I was just your little sister's best friend, and I always had been. I had no way of knowing you ever felt anything different about me."

"Why would you?" he asked with a wry smile. "I was your best friend's annoying brother. Like I could tell you."

"So why did you finally do it?"

"You pushed me. You kept demanding to know who my perfect girl was without knowing that I was looking right at her. So... I kissed you." He shrugged, looking at the floor. "Probably should have just used a thing called words, in hindsight, but never mind."

The lump in my throat was almost painful. I couldn't swallow it to save my life. "Do you regret it?"

He jerked his head up, his gaze slamming into mine. "No. I told you yesterday. I could never regret you, Chlo. And even if you don't want to do this, I'll only regret that I never had the balls to tell you sooner."

"I don't know what to do," I said softly. "We fight. All the time. About everything. This is the only conversation I feel like we've had in two weeks where we haven't been fighting with each other. That's not healthy. No matter how many times you switch my pens or check the printer ink or do all those other things. All I ever do for you is save you the last slice of pizza."

His lips twitched to one side. "You save me the last slice of pizza?"

I shrugged, sitting up straight, but still hugging my knee. "Yeah. You used to steal it all the time, and I guess, at some point, I just started leaving it. Doesn't matter if it were fresh or twelve hours old and been sitting there all night. I know you'll check the box, so... I leave it."

Dom titled his head to the side. "I dunno. Saving someone pizza is about as close to true love as a person can get."

Quietly, I laughed, dipping my chin to my chest. That was true. Pizza and bacon were the foods of love. Screw chocolate. I wanted someone to bring me a plate of bacon for Valentine's Day.

My laugh petered out, and when I looked back up, he was still smiling. "Why are you smiling at me like that?"

"Can't a guy smile at the person he's in love with?"

"I guess he can."

His smile turned into a smirk before it dropped, and he walked over to me. He swung my chair around, so I faced him, then brushed hair from my face. "Come on, Chlo. Let's try. What do we have to lose?"

"Everything." I wheeled my chair back and stood up, wrapping one arm around my waist. "If it doesn't work, we don't just lose each other; we potentially lose all of this." I waved my hand around my office. "We won't be able to go back to how it was."

"How it was isn't gonna change." He stood, hands out. "What, you think I'm suddenly gonna stop losing my keys, and you're gonna stop yelling at me about them? Or you're gonna stop getting annoyed because I didn't pay the internet company on time? Or you're going to stop passively aggressively muttering to yourself in the kitchen because I didn't take the used coffee pod out of the coffee machine?"

"I do not do that."

"I have literally stood next to the door to listen to you do it."

"Fine. I did it once."

"I did it three times."

"I don't know what point you're trying to make here, but it's starting to annoy me."

Dom grinned. "See? It'll never stop. I don't want it to stop. It's who we are. We bicker over stupid stuff, but has any of those fights ever changed the way you feel about me?"

I opened my mouth and—nothing. Nothing came out.

Because no. No, it hadn't. Not once.

Smugness took over his smile. "See? You yelling at me and calling me all the names under the sun on a weekly basis never changed how I wanted you or how I loved it. And you're missing the big picture."

"Which is what, exactly?"

"I don't want to stop fighting with you, Chlo. If we stop fighting, it means we've stopped caring. Even about the little things."

I took a deep breath. It escaped with a shudder because I knew he was right. All the things we fought about, even the ridiculously stupid stuff, was because we cared.

"And, listen to me." He walked toward me, stopping right in front of me, and raised one hand to my face. His palm was soft and warm against my cheek, and I bit the inside of my lip. "You don't have to be afraid of us not working. There's not a chance in hell that would ever happen. You'd kill me before we ever broke up."

"Eh." I shrugged. "Probably true."

"Besides. I don't even like you most of the time—"

"Gee, thanks, Romeo."

"—But that doesn't change the fact I can't see myself spending the rest of my life with anyone other than you."

"Which, in all honesty, will probably be very short. As soon as I have your life insurance policy in place."

Dom stepped back and gave a mock bow. "I've already been pricing quotes for you. How about that for true love, eh?"

"Save me the last slice of pizza, then we'll talk." I crossed my arms over my chest. "I don't know. I need to think about it."

He threw his arms in the air, running one hand through his hair on its way back down. "No. You don't. You'll just overthink it."

"I will not!"

"You will! I've watched you overthink adding ham to your pizza in the past!"

"Pizza is serious business!"

Dom rubbed his hand down his face. "I didn't wanna do this, but I'm playing dirty."

I did a double-take. "Excuse me?"

"We made a deal. Three dates with someone of the other's choosing."

Oh no.

"Both of us only went on one date."

"Wait, but—"

"I'm setting you up with me." He mimicked my standing by folding his arms. "And you owe me two dates to finish out this little experiment."

"That's not fair!"

He grinned, smugly. His eyes twinkled with silent laughter as they met mine. "Two dates. You owe me to get out of our little agreement."

"Fine. But I'm not setting you up with me."

"Doesn't matter, Little Miss Stubborn. I already called it. You're locked in."

"I'm busy every night," I huffed.

He shrugged. "So, we'll go for breakfast."

"I don't eat breakfast."

"Lunch, then."

"I have plans."

"Right now, then."

"I'm bus—"

He cut me off with one sleek movement. His hand cupped the back of my head and his lips covered mine in a way that gave me no choice but to shut up and stop arguing with me.

And God, it felt so good.

Soft and warm with just enough pressure to make my hair stand on end.

"Now, you're busy," he whispered against my lips.

The break in the kiss lasted only a second before he continued. Slow and tender, his teeth grazed my lower lip as both his hands cupped my face. My fingers crept toward his t-shirt, winding themselves into the soft cotton as I did the inevitable and gave in to him.

Until there was a rousing knock-knock-knock at the door, and we jumped apart as if we'd just been caught making out under the bleachers.

Dom grinned, cupping my chin.

My eyes focused on the corner of his mouth. "You have, uh…" I rubbed my thumb against his skin.

"Lipstick. Here." I pulled a packet of makeup removal wipes from my desk drawer and handed them to him. "Use one of these."

He pulled one out and gave a thorough wipe of his mouth. "Better?"

I nodded.

"Now, go fix yours." With a wink, he went to answer the door, and I ran into the bathroom, wipes in hand.

One look in the mirror, and I needed more than a fix.

I needed a total re-do.

***

This. Was. Ridiculous.

He'd all but corralled me into two dates with him, and he was right. It was playing dirty, because he knew I wouldn't back out of it. He knew I'd agreed, and part of the problem with growing up with Peyton Austin as your best friend was the uncanny ability to never back out of a challenge.

She was the most competitive person I knew, even more so than Dom. Unfortunately for me, they'd grown up competing against each other, and I knew there was no way out of this.

No matter how I felt or what I wanted, I had to go on two dates with Dom.

And deep down inside, I was as giddy as could be. Terrified, sure, but giddy as fuck. Truth was, I wanted to go out with him. I wanted to go on a date with him and see if this could work. If we could really let our feelings control our relationship in a new way.

I was still skeptical. Sure, he'd told me we would work, but he wasn't a psychic. He had no way of knowing whether or not we'd be together in ten years, but a part of me wanted to find out.

It wanted me to believe him.

I wanted him to be right. Above all else, I was in love with him, and I wanted to be with him. Even if I did kill him one day. I wouldn't even deny it, but there'd be no doubt everyone on the jury would agree he deserved it.

There was no doubt he'd deserve it if I ever murdered him.

I probably would if he ever did it to me.

Anyone who ever said you don't kill the things you love never met Dominic Austin.

I took a deep breath and looked in the mirror. My hair was dry, but my body was still wrapped in a towel. I had no idea what his plans for tonight were, just that we were going on a date and I had to be ready by six-thirty.

It was six-fifteen.

It wasn't looking promising.

How did we get here? How did this all get so complicated? It should be straightforward. That's how it is in the movies. Everyone confesses they love each other, then they go for a nice, candlelit dinner, and then they have all the sex.

Was that what the plan for tonight was?

I wasn't prepared for a candlelit dinner. I didn't have the patience for it. Plus, I'd eaten an entire jumbo bag of Cheetos for a late afternoon snack, and that was clearly a mistake.

I groaned and dropped back onto the bed. I bounced a few times on the mattress and blew out a long breath. What was wrong with me?

Could I get out of this? How? When? I was running out of time.

I didn't—

Knock, knock, knock.

I sat bolt upright.

No.

No, no, no. Was he early? Didn't he know women were always late? We had at least a ten-minute leeway before it was considered rude. He wasn't allowed to be ten minutes early.

Shit the bed and call me Sally, I was in trouble.

But, wait. What if it wasn't Dom? What if it was someone else, and I was wrapped in a towel that was very close to showing off my vagina?

I clutched at the towel and tentatively made my way downstairs. Another round of knocking sounded, and I hovered in the doorway to the kitchen. The unclear reflection through the wavy glass looked like Dom, so I took a punt and opened the front door.

Thank God.

It was Dom.

His dark eyes roved over me from head to toe. "Do you always answer the door in a barely-there towel?"

"Only to people I've slept with," I quipped.

"Are there many of those?"

"I could tell you, but then I'd have to kill you." I grinned.

He did not. "You're not dressed."

"You're early," I fired back. "I'm almost ready."

He dropped his eyes to my legs. "Chloe, you're not even wet. How long have you been wrapped in that towel?"

"Long enough to dry off naturally, evidently." I adjusted the towel at my chest again. "You're still early. You're not supposed to be here until twenty 'til."

"I said six-thirty." He raised an eyebrow.

"You didn't include my obligatory extra ten minutes. I'm a woman. It's almost guaranteed I'll need to pee right before we leave."

"Oh, good. You're an adult-sized toddler."

I pursed my lips. "If you were hoping to get laid tonight, calling me a toddler isn't a step in the right direction."

Dom put his hands in his jeans pockets, lips tugging into a smile. "Is getting laid on the cards?"

"Not anymore."

"That's all right. I'll always have my memories."

I rolled my eyes as he laughed. "How dressed up do I need to be?"

He waved one hand down himself before stuffing it back into his pocket. "Just be comfortable. And by comfortable, I don't mean yoga pants."

"Do I have to wear a bra?"

"Yes. I don't want you scaring away any children."

I glared at him. He was such a dick.

"Also, you said sex was off the table, so you going braless doesn't help me at all."

I sighed and turned for the stairs. "I'm regretting this already."

"I can see up your towel."

I reached behind me and held the towel against my butt. I didn't think it made the blindest bit of difference—at least that's what I got from his endless laughter—but it made me feel better.

"I can still see!"

Goddamn it.

CHAPTER EIGHTEEN

.

CHLOE

Not all dates are created equal.
Just ask Miss Rhode Island from Miss Congeniality.
April 25th is the perfect date.
That one where someone tells you his ex-wife's life story?
Not so much.

"WHAT ARE YOU DOING?"

"Shh. I can't hear." I leaned a little to the left to hear the conversation of the couple on the bench closest to me.

Dom sat down with two plastic bags full of food. "Seriously. What are you doing?"

"The couple behind us are on a date," I whispered. "And he keeps talking about his ex-wife. Seriously. It doesn't stop."

"You're also on a date, and you're more interested in theirs."

I sighed and looked at him. "Where did you get the food?"

He nodded toward a small Cajun restaurant on the other side of the park. "I made a deal with Josie. I'll help her find a date for free if she gave me a take-out before they technically start doing them."

I raised an eyebrow. "I think I'm a little impressed."

"You should be. I owe her three months of free help. And I had to pay for the food."

"You must be horrified. How will you cope?"

"You could take off your bra."

"No can do. There are still kids around."

He laughed and pulled containers out of the bags onto the blanket we were sitting on. "I didn't know what you wanted, so I got a whole bunch of stuff."

"Okay."

"You're still trying to listen to their conversation, aren't you?"

"I see a business opportunity," I lied. "We could help that girl."

"Chloe, you're not going a great job on your own date."

"I know, but I'm really good at it for other people."
I gave him a cheesy smile.

"You can't just pluck random people off the street.
Especially not if you don't have business cards with
you."

I paused. "Would it be acceptable if I did have
business cards?"

Dom paused, halfway through opening some rice.
"You have business cards with you?"

I patted my purse. "I always keep business cards
with me. You never know when you might need them.
Like now." Another sweet grin stretched across my lips.

He put down the tub of rice and stared at me. With
a completely straight face, he said, "You know what? If
I wasn't already in love with you, this would go down as
the worst date ever."

I pointed at him. "You started that when you
showed up early."

He waved his hands. "Still not acceptable to hijack
someone's date to tout our business."

I pouted.

"If she leaves first, chase her. If he leaves, grab one
of the donuts from the other bag and drop it so you can
slip a card in her purse." He grinned, reaching for the
other bag. He pulled out a small, brown paper bag.
"Just in case."

I opened the bag and saw a bunch of mini donuts
inside. My lips curved to the side as I peered up at him
through my lashes.

Huh.

Maybe this wasn't so insane after all. I mean, he got
me, didn't he? He understood how my mind worked.

And maybe it was totally crazy to tout our services to a random woman on a bad date—all right, there was no maybe about it—but it was fun.

"He's leaving," Dom muttered. "Quick, get me a card."

"What are you going to do?"

"I'm going to flirt the card into her purse."

I bristled. "You are not."

He grinned. "Does that annoy you?"

I glared at him. "I have a better idea." I dug through my purse to find the stack of cards I kept in a holder. I slipped one out and, holding it between my fingers, wiggled it at him. "I'll be right back."

"Weirdest fucking date ever," he said under his breath as I jumped up.

"Heard that."

"Good."

I shook my head and tentatively approached the young woman on the bench. "Hi," I said.

She turned toward me, her frustrated look turning to one of confusion. "Hi. Do I know you?"

"No…. Do you mind if I join you for a moment? Or is your date coming back?"

"Lord, I hope not." She motioned to the bench and smoothed her dark, frizzy hair back from her face. "Take a seat."

"Thanks. Bad date?" I sat down.

"The worst. All he talked about was his ex-wife. How she'd claimed custody of the dog he owned before her, how she was claiming support she wasn't entitled to, how he knew she cheated on him but couldn't prove it and yadda yadda yadda." She rolled dark eyes.

"Whatever. I'm so over this, you know? How hard is it to find someone who can have a nice dinner with you?"

"Well, that's actually why I approached you," I said hesitantly. "I overheard your conversation with him, and I felt so bad for you."

She eyed me skeptically.

"My name is Chloe, and I own the dating company, Stupid Cupid."

Her mouth opened. "Oh! I've heard of you! My friend used you, but I was wary."

I couldn't help but smile. "Here. Take my card. Just say I spoke to you in the park, and I can book you in for a free consultation."

"Really?" Her face lit up.

"Really."

She took the card. "Thanks. That's so kind. I'm Hannah."

"Nice to meet you." We shared a smile. "I have to get back to my date, but we'll speak soon?"

"You skipped your date to give me this?"

I shrugged a shoulder. "He's my business partner. He had a vested interest in this."

She laughed and nodded. "We'll speak soon, then."

I got up, waved, and went back over to Dom. He had a mouthful of shrimp when I joined him.

"'Ell?" he asked me.

I wrinkled my face. "Do you always speak to your dates with your mouth full of food?"

"Only the ones I've slept with," he said, smirking at me. "Well? Did she take it?"

"You didn't watch?"

He scoffed. "No. I was hungry, and you were taking too long."

"Your manners suck." I picked up another tray of shrimp and a plastic fork. "Yes, she took it. I offered her a free consultation if she said we spoke in the park. Her name is Hannah."

"Hey, that's not a bad idea," Dom said, pointing his fork at me. "Free consultations."

I inclined my head toward him. I had a mouthful of food, and I wasn't nearly as rude as he was. I swallowed, then said, "You know what would be fun?"

"I don't think I want to," he replied slowly.

I put down my food and leaned forward. "We should look for people on bad dates and give them our cards!"

"That sounds like a terrible idea."

"Why? We give them free consultations, but they have to pay to be matched if we can find them a date. It's genius, Dom!"

"I wish I'd never said the consultations were a good idea," he groaned. "Chloe..."

"Oh, come on. It'd be fun!"

"We have different ideas of fun."

"Of course, we do." I flipped my hair over my shoulder. "You spent your teen years with Playboy in your bedroom while I was out having a life."

Dom put the lid back on his carton of food and looked at me out of the corner of his eye. "You also spent your teen years in love with me."

"As you apparently did me."

He paused. "Touché. Fine. We'll play your little game, but if we don't find two people in the next thirty minutes, we're doing something else."

"Like what?"

"I don't know, but I'll think of something. We'll go bug hunting or some shit. Anything but this."

"Bug hunting?" I stilled. "I don't like bugs."

"I don't like forcing my business onto unsuspecting people."

"Are you kidding? They'll love it. They can go dating with a custom-found date? Not one matched by computers? It's genius."

"You told me that when we set the business up, but all that got me is a few years of blue balls over you."

"Carry on annoying me, and I'll turn them purple."

"How?"

"I'll put them in a blender with a bowl full of plums, that's how." I covered the last carton and put it in the bag. "Let's put these in your car and go and have some fun!"

He groaned, collecting the blanket from the grass. "You're lucky you're hot."

"That's pretty much the only reason I'm still alive," I said. "It gets me out of trouble."

He side-eyed me. "Someone's ego is getting out of control."

"From the guy who claims he always gives a woman three orgasms during sex."

Dom froze. "Are you saying you didn't have three?"

I held up two fingers, walking backward, and grinned. "Sucker."

He looked at me darkly—full of desire. He drew level with me and hooked one finger through one of my belt loops. "Probably just as well. You screamed so loud at the end of the second, I was expecting the dead to walk through your front door."

I pursed my lips. "Yeah, well, I'm probably better equipped to deal with it than you are."

"Chloe, you couldn't walk."

"I can throw a mean punch."

Dom shook his head. "Nothing about you is mean when you have Bambi legs."

I stopped dead on the path and shot him a massive glare that would have killed a lesser person.

He stilled. "All right, that would probably work. Let's move on, shall we?"

"You're smarter than you look, Dominic."

"I don't know if that's a compliment or not."

I shrugged. "You'll have to figure that one out."

***

"Don't take this the wrong way," I said to Dom when he returned to our table. "But you are a terrible flirter."

His eyebrows raised as he slid onto the stool opposite me. "What? No, I'm not. I'm a great flirter."

"You're really not. Remember how I was all against you flirting with the girl in the park?"

He nodded.

"Flirt with whoever you want. I've never seen anyone as bad at it as you."

He picked up his beer and sipped. "How am I a bad flirter?"

"Well, for a start, you're awkward. You make too much eye contact without actually looking at her, and you just seem, I don't know." I twirled one of my curls around my finger. "Awkward."

"You already said that," he said tightly.

"If I'm saying it twice, it's true." I shrugged a shoulder. "At the very least you should have touched her arm once."

"That's creepy."

"No. It's nice. It shows you're interested."

He put his beer down. "But I'm not interested."

I rolled my eyes. "But you want her to think you are."

He folded his arms across his chest. "All right. There's a guy at the bar whose date just stepped outside to take a phone call. He looks miserable."

I scanned the bar. "The guy taking the shot?"

He looked over his shoulder. "Yeah. If you're such a flirting expert, go flirt our card into his pocket."

"You're not gonna like this," I warned him. "I'm an excellent flirter."

"I'm sure you are," he drawled. "Go on, then. Show me how it's done. I'll try to contain my jealousy."

Oh, ye of little faith.

This was about to get really awkward.

"All right, then." I slipped a card into my back pocket and got up. He was still alone at the bar, so I moseyed on over and paused behind the stool. "Is this seat taken?"

The guy turned to me, giving me the once-over. "Supposed to be, but she's having a long-ass phone conversation."

"I just want to get a drink. Do you mind?"

He shook his head. "Knock yourself out, darlin'."

"Thank you so much!" I shot him my brightest smile and slid onto the stool, making sure my knee brushed his leg as I did so. "Oh, sorry. I didn't mean to hit you."

"No," he said slowly, eyes firmly on me. "You're all good."

Again, another smile, then I turned and focused on getting the bartender's attention. "Bad date, huh?"

"That obvious?"

"Well, I just watched you down three shots, and judging by how long she's been outside, I don't think she's coming back."

"I think you could be right, blondie." He held up two fingers, finally grabbing the bartender's attention. "What're you drinking?"

"I'll have a white wine, but I can get that." I put two fingers into my back pocket and pulled out both a ten-dollar bill and the business card. I tossed both onto the bar, then paused. "Woops."

"Wait, what was that?" He touched my hand, tilting it toward him so he could see the card.

"What can I get you?" The bartender leaned over to us.

"I'll have a Coors Light, and she'll have a white wine," the guy said.

"A dry white. Thanks." I smiled and turned back to the guy whose name I didn't know. "The card?"

"Yeah. What is it?"

I wriggled my hand from his grip and slid it in front of him, leaning in slightly. "It's a card for a dating service. Why?"

"A dating service? You used it?" He looked interested as he plucked it from my fingers.

"Actually," I blushed as I tucked hair behind my ear. "I co-own it."

"You do?"

"Yeah. I carry the cards because, well, I'm a businesswoman, and you wouldn't believe how many bars and restaurants will take these things." I smiled and went to take it back.

He moved it out of my reach. "You any good?"

"I like to think so, but I'm also pretty bias. Thank you," I added to the bartender, sliding my money across the bar. "Why? You interested?"

The guy nodded toward the door. "I'm not doing a fucking good job by myself, am I?"

"How was it going before she went out?"

"She wouldn't stop talking about her degree. If I knew she was in college, I wouldn't have asked her out. She told me she was twenty-five. Turns out, she's twenty-one."

Ouch.

"How old are you?"

"Twenty-eight. Why? Are you hitting on me?"

I laughed and touched his arm. "Do you want me to be?"

"Depends. Are you in college?" It was his turn to laugh.

"No. I definitely graduated, thank God. Why don't you keep that card? Give me a call. You can come into my office for a free consultation, and I'll personally match you with someone. How does that sound?"

He tilted his head to the side. He was definitely considering it.

"Come on," I said, leaning in. "I'm giving you a consultation for free. What do you have to lose?"

Right then, the door opened, and when I glanced up, I saw his date stepping through the door.

"Think about it," I said, picking up my glass and standing, slipping past him back to my table.

Dom glared at me as I sat down. "What was that?"

"It was effective flirting. I told you that you wouldn't like it. It's not my fault if you didn't believe me."

He slid onto the stool next to me. "Did you have to get so close to him?"

Was it bad I was enjoying this? All those years of seeing women flirt with him...

"Yes. That was the entire point. He took the business card when I accidentally pulled it out of my pocket."

He grunted.

I pinched his cheek. "Aww. What? Was I right?"

He glared at me again, eyes dark and annoyed, and grabbed my stool. He pulled the stool toward him until our seats bumped, then cupped the back of my head and kissed me.

Hard.

"What was that?" I asked when he pulled back.

"I saw the way he looked at you, and I don't like it," he muttered.

"You don't like it?" I couldn't help the twitching of my lips.

"Why would I? You're mine."

I leaned back, raising my eyebrows. "I'm yours?"

He nodded. "You're mine."

"I'm not the last pair of shoes in your size in the store, Dominic."

"What's your point? You'd be mine even if you were."

I folded my arms. "I'm not a possession."

"Funny. Now that I think about it, you were pretty possessive when Ruby walked into the office."

"Don't you dare throw her back in my face."

"You were so jealous. Do you remember that? You were all up in my business about how inappropriate she was and wondering if I found her on a street corner. Remember?" His eyes sparkled as he said it, and that gave it away.

I knew what he was doing, and I wasn't going to bite.

"I remember," I said flatly, taking a sip of my wine. "She was so desperate the local wildlife could smell her."

"You really hated her."

Still do.

"I'm surprised you didn't claw her eyes out."

"Dom, your game is so obvious, the local Kindergarten has already rolled their dice and won. Quit it. I don't care about her." I met his eyes. "If you're trying to bug me, it's not working."

"You sound bugged."

"You sound like you want me to conclude that we'll never work."

"Yet, here you are, fighting with me." He brought his beer to his lips. "Because you're annoyed that I'm trying to make you jealous because you know you are."

I took a big gulp of wine. "Stick your psychological bullshit up your ass, Dr. Phil."

"You're just proving my point."

"I'm going to leave in a second."

"I'll follow you."

"I'll punch you," I warned him. "I've done it before. I hit you with a wooden spoon, remember?"

He winced. "Yes, and it hurt. But you don't have a spoon."

"I have a purse."

"Calm down, Grandma."

"All right. I'm leaving." I stood up, but he swept one arm around my waist and pulled me right back down.

"No, you're not," he said, holding me against his side. "Might I remind you that this was your idea? You're the one who wanted to find single people on bad dates. He was the first guy we've found. You can't be mad at me for getting jealous when he's looking at you like you're a piece of cake."

"Please. He didn't look at me like I was a piece of cake."

"If he had a spoon, he'd have eaten you."

"I'm a cheesecake. I'm too good to be normal cake. He'd need a fork for that."

Dom turned his head and looked at me. "I don't know how to respond to that."

"You're not supposed to. I've told you before—I have a superior wit. It's my weapon. Taking people off-guard with my brilliance."

"Brilliance? I think you're full of shit."

"I know. But you like my shit." I paused. "I mean, my witty shit. Not my actual shit."

"I'm so glad you clarified," he said in a droll tone. "I couldn't possibly figure out what the hell you meant."

"I'm here to help."

He tightened his grip on me, pulling me closer into him. We might have been sitting on backless stools, but he had such a solid grip on me, it barely felt like it. I was tucked almost perfectly against the curve of his side, and I rested my head on his shoulder.

It felt right.

Like I fit against his body perfectly. Like his arms were the perfect size and length to wrap around me and hold me against him. Like there was no other place I should have been.

No other place I was ever meant to be.

I tilted my face into him. "Dom?"

"Hmm?"

"Take me home."

CHAPTER NINETEEN

DOM

Not all love stories were perfect.
Some people snored.
Like Chloe.

CHLOE DUG HER KEYS OUT OF HER PURSE AND UNLOCKED her front door. It swung open with one gentle push, and she stepped inside, clicking a switch and filling the hallway with light.

Her street was otherwise almost completely dark. There were no streetlights except at the very ends on the main roads, and since she lived in the middle, all she was illuminated by was the dim hall light and that of one porch light to the right of her door.

She turned, dropping her purse strap off her shoulder and down her arm until it rested in her hand. "Aren't you coming in?"

I leaned against the pillar that held up the small balcony off her bedroom. "Do you want me to come in?"

"Do you want to?" She drew her lower lip between her teeth, and the apprehension in her eyes hit me.

She was nervous.

"I want to," I said softly. "But I don't have to."

"I want you to." She stepped back, opening the doorway for me. "I don't have any pizza for you, though."

"I think I'll cope." I followed her inside and shut the door behind me. She slipped against me, putting the key in the hole and twisting it. "Did you just lock me in?" I asked her.

"No. You're free to leave at any time. All you have to do is twist the key." She stepped away, hovering awkwardly. "Can I be honest?"

"I'd welcome that."

She twisted her hands in front of her, dipping her head slightly so that her blonde curls covered her beautiful face. "I don't..." She lifted her face to meet my eyes. "I didn't invite you in to have sex."

I didn't say anything. I knew that.

"I had fun tonight. A lot of fun. And... we didn't fight."

"We bickered, Chlo."

"We didn't yell," she corrected. "And, I don't know. What happens if you stay, but we don't have sex? Will that ruin anything?"

"Well, that depends. Are you gonna make me watch *Friends*? Or can we both decide on a TV show to watch? Because, you know. I've seen enough of that show to last me a lifetime."

"That depends, too. Are we naked in bed watching with ice cream?"

"As a rule, yes. Yes, we are."

"We don't have to watch *Friends*," she said. "But I'm not watching a totally man-ish show, either. How about a movie?"

"A movie sounds good. What haven't you seen?"

"The new Avengers."

I paused. "You only want to watch that for Hemsworth."

Chloe pulled a tub of ice cream out of the freezer and shot me a look. "And you'll watch it for Scarlett Johansson. What's your point?"

I didn't have one.

"Let's watch that." I grabbed two spoons from the drawer. "Upstairs?"

She nodded. "Let's go. I can deal with this." She ran up the stairs, a tub of ice cream in hand, and I followed her. She was already getting undressed with her back to me by the time I made it into the bedroom, and I paused to watch her.

She was fucking beautiful. From her blonde curls to the bean-shaped birthmark on her lower back.

She paused. "Are you watching me?"

"No. I'm… looking out of the window."

"So, I'm now transparent and square. Awesome." She turned to me and put her hands on her hips. "Why are you still clothed?"

"I was busy looking out the window," I said, putting the spoons on the bed. I pulled my shirt over my head and kicked off my shoes simultaneously. I didn't miss the way she unabashedly stared at me as I undressed.

"Now who's staring?"

"Shut up." She reached over the bed, grabbing the spoons and climbed under the covers. It took her seconds to pull off the lid of the Ben and Jerry's tub. She dug her spoon in before I'd even unzipped my pants, for the love of God.

"Thanks for waiting for me," I muttered, kicking off my jeans and sitting on the bed next to her.

"Ice cream waits for nobody," she said, spoon in her mouth, and reached for the TV remote.

"Ice cream, or you?" I questioned, pulling the covers over me.

"Ice cream," she said, looking at me. "It melts. Duh."

She had me there.

"It's hard to argue with that kind of logic." I leaned over and stuck my spoon in the tub. Pushing down into the ice cream, her grip loosened, and she let go of the tub.

"Hey!"

I took it and pulled a huge chunk out of the ice cream.

She stared, slack-jawed, at the tub. "Why would you do that?"

"How else am I supposed to eat it?" I questioned, putting the spoon in my mouth.

"Slowly and gently."

"It's ice cream. Not a kitten."

"It's the best ice cream," Chloe said, snatching the tub back. "You can't just dive into Ben and Jerry's like a savage. You have to treat it with respect."

"Again," I said slowly, "It's ice cream, not a kitten."

She looked down at the tub then back up at me. "This might be a deal-breaker for me."

"I think you're insane."

"Is that how you treat someone who saves you the last piece of pizza?"

I paused. "It is when they think ice cream is something to be revered."

"You're getting real close to sleeping on the floor tonight, Dominic."

"Is that so you can sleep with the ice cream?"

She stared at me. "Yes. At least it won't talk back to me like you do. Or eat my last piece of pizza. In fact, I think I'll be in a relationship with Ben and Jerry's instead of you."

I stopped.

She froze. Her eyes widened, and I swear she nearly choked on her own saliva. "I mean—not that we're, you know. I didn't... shit."

I fought back a laugh. "I really want to jump in here, so you don't dig yourself a deeper hole with that statement, but I want to see you talk your way out of it."

She licked her lips. "I didn't, um." She pushed her hair away from her face and stared at the wall.

I took the tub of ice cream and started eating. She was too traumatized by what she'd let slip—the big, scary 'r' word—to even notice that I was tearing chunks out of the tub.

"I can still see you being mean to my ice cream," she said in a small voice.

Maybe she did notice.

Three spoonfuls of ice cream later, she finally turned back to look at me. "I didn't mean to imply that we were in a relationship. Because, you know. We haven't said that."

"Well, that sucks, then," I said and licked my spoon. "Because I just assumed we were starting one."

"You assumed?"

"You agreed to go out with me."

She shifted so her body was facing me. "I did not agree. I was coerced into it. There's a difference."

"So, this is the modern-day Beauty and the Beast, just without the kidnapping. Hey, wasn't that your favorite movie as a kid?" I pointed the spoon at her.

"What does that have to do with this?"

"Nothing. It just came to mind. Was it?"

"Yes, but—"

"Now, you're Belle. Coerced into dating me. You're lucky I have a great sense of humor and an even better cock. And way less hairy than Beast."

She blinked at me. "I don't know how to respond to that."

"You could agree." I grinned.

"No. I don't think you need the ego boost, in all honesty. And you're taking this conversation off-track. Don't think I'm going to let you get away with saying I agreed to date you."

"All right, I won't say it. But I will say that you happily invited me to your bed with ice cream."

"And I'll tell everyone I promptly followed that up by considering kicking you out and replacing you *with* the ice cream."

"Most people would probably be more horrified that you threatened it and didn't do it. I'd rather sleep with ice cream than with me." I shrugged a shoulder and pulled out another chunk of the chocolate treat.

She snatched the tub back. "Stop abusing my ice cream, you savage."

"Are you still in a relationship with it, or are you and I back on?"

"I never said we were on."

"Your denial of everything makes me ridiculously happy."

Chloe's brows drew together in a frown. "Why does me refusing to admit to being in a relationship with you make you happy?"

"Because, when you eventually admit it, I'll be right. And I'm pretty fond of being right." I grinned. "So, you may as well just admit it now."

"And make you right?"

"Get it over and done with. What? Are you gonna marry me and never admit to being in a relationship with me?"

"Who said I was going to marry you?" Her voice was close to a shriek.

I put the ice cream on the side and leaned back against the headboard. "Well, you're getting a little close to thirty now, and time isn't on your side."

She stared at me incredulously. "If you're trying to win me over, you're not doing very well."

Fuck. It was hard not to laugh. "I mean, your tits won't be this perky forever. Are they as lively as they used to be?"

Her jaw dropped.

"And your ass won't always be this free of cellulite. Never mind going gray. I mean, I'm willing to take all this on as a part of you, but—"

"Asshole!" She laughed, launching herself at me. She punched me in the arm and, laughing, I moved away from her and off the bed. She jumped off it, coming after me. I ran around the other side of the bed, holding out my hands.

"Careful. There's still no life insurance policy. You don't wanna beat me up too bad."

Chloe narrowed her eyes. "I could kill you right now, but I do want to benefit from your death."

"Which is why you're an excellent businesswoman. Terrible girlfriend, but great at your job."

"I'm not your girlfriend."

"Chloe. We both know you're my girlfriend. At least, you will be tomorrow morning after you've had my pancakes."

She paused, dropping her fists. "You can make pancakes?"

"Yeah," I said slowly. "It's not hard."

"Huh. I can never get those right," she mused. "But I'm still not your girlfriend."

"And your tits still aren't getting any perkier."

"Jerkface!" She jumped on the bed and, once again, threw herself at me.

This time, I was able to catch her.

I grabbed hold of her as she pummeled my shoulders with her fists.

"Put me down!" she shouted.

"No." I spun and dropped onto the bed, bringing her with me. She shrieked, grabbing my shoulders instead of punching them.

I much preferred the grabbing. She had one hell of a right hand, even when she was punching me like a three-year-old.

"Why did you do that?" she demanded. She flattened her hands on the bed on either side of my head and looked down at me. Her hair fell forward around her face, tickling me on the cheek.

"It made you stop hitting me, didn't it?" I asked, eyebrow quirked.

"Can I carry on now?"

"No."

"Will you let me go then?"

"No. Not until you admit that you're my girlfriend."

"You sound very high school," she muttered.

I rolled us over so she was under me. I straddled her, grabbing her hands and pinning her to the bed so that she couldn't wriggle away from me. "Admit it."

"No."

"We both know it's going to happen."

"Real cocky for a guy who has to pin me down and coerce me into dates."

"I told you earlier. I'm fine with playing dirty." I gave her a lopsided grin and leaned down, bringing my face closer to hers. "Plus, you and I both know you're just being awkward. I know just how long you've been in love with me, Chloe Collins."

"Do you, now? And how did you find that out?" She tilted her chin up.

"Peyton has a big mouth."

"Gonna kill her," she muttered.

I snorted, sliding my hands over hers and linking our fingers. "You're gonna get one hell of a jail sentence."

"It'll be worth it."

I smiled, looking into her eyes. "Just admit it, Chlo. You're hopelessly in love with me, and there's no chance in hell that you're going to walk away from giving us a chance."

"I'll give you the first one," she said softly. "I am pretty screwed where my emotions are concerned regarding you."

"That's the nicest way anyone has ever told me they love me. You should write romance."

Her lips twitched, and her eyes twinkled for a moment before she tilted her head to the side and let out a giggle. "I'm not entirely sure I would be good at that. I mean, it took me twenty-seven years to get to this point."

"On the plus side, you are a pro at being in love. That's some practice you've had."

She pursed her lips. "You're not exactly a love virgin yourself, are you? You've been in love with me for at least ten years."

"Who told you—" I stopped. "Never mind. I think I can probably guess it was Peyton."

She nodded. "She has a big mouth. I guess she got the mouth and you got the ego."

"Well, could you imagine if she had both? She'd be a nightmare."

"As opposed to the delight she currently is." Chloe snorted. "Can you let me up now?"

"No." I flexed my fingers between hers. "Not until you give me what I want."

"Well," she said. "I can't give you a blow job if I'm up here and your cock is down there."

Hmm. Tempting.

"As great as that sounds, that's not what I mean." I dipped my head and kissed just beneath her ear. She drew in a short, sharp breath, and I knew.

This was how to break her down.

To admit what she already knew.

That despite all her fighting, she was mine. There were no two ways about it. She'd been mine for years.

At least her heart had been mine, just like it was right now.

"Admit it," I murmured against her skin. "You're mine, Chloe. You know it. You're fighting the inevitable." I kissed along her jaw until my lips reached the corner of her mouth. "Just give in."

"Never," she whispered.

"Fine, awkward one," I said, kissing her jaw again. "But I'm yours. Me. My heart. And all my lost keys."

She groaned. "And that's a lot of keys."

"At least ten in the last two years. And now..." I looked her in the eye. "You get to witness me lose them forever. Aren't you lucky?"

"We have different meanings for the word lucky," she replied. "Do you really think we can make this work?"

"I know we can," I said honestly. "Is it gonna be easy? No. Are we gonna fight? Hopefully. The more we fight, the more make-up sex we get."

"That is promising," she mused.

"More than anything, I want to make it work. And I know you do, too, or you wouldn't even be here entertaining it right now." I released her hand and brushed hair from her face. "Am I perfect? No. Am I gonna piss you off? Sure. But, Chlo? That's no different to the relationship we have right now. The only difference is that now, we know we love each other. We didn't have that before."

"If you're trying to tell me that you losing your keys is going to turn into something cute instead of insufferably annoying, you're very wrong," she warned me.

"Is there not even a hint of a chance with that?"

"Not a chance in hell."

"I'm okay with you shouting at me for that."

"I'd be more okay if you tried to not lose them in the first place."

I grinned. "I can work on that," I said.

She looked at me, lips pursed, but I knew she was agreeing. I could see it in her eyes. "I guess I can work on my temper."

"Does that mean you'll give me the chance to—shock horror—explain myself?" I gasped, pressing my hand to my chest.

She hit me. "You're not starting this well, Dom."

"Starting? Does that mean I win? I've worn you down?"

"Actually, I think I just want you to shut up about it," she teased, half-grinning. "That, and I have a teenage girl inside throwing a party," she added.

I couldn't help the grin that stretched across my face. "So, you're agreeing to be my girlfriend?"

"I'll agree officially when you've made me pancakes."

"Is that because you can't make them?"

"Hey," she said, raising her eyebrows. "Food matters. I like pancakes. You can make pancakes. I'm not against letting food make the final choice for me."

"That sounds a hell of a lot like something I'd say. Maybe you really are the perfect girl for me."

"Stop being nice. You're scaring me."

I laughed and brushed my lips over hers. "I promise to revert to annoying you in the morning."

"Thank you. I think keeping our relationship just as it is might be the success to this after all."

"I completely agree," I murmured, lowering my lips to hers.

She wrapped her free arm around my neck and kissed me back, flicking her tongue against the seam of my lips. I let go of her hand, and that arm joined her other, pulling me right down against her so I couldn't escape.

Pancakes my ass.

She was mine, and she knew it.

And my God, we were going to make this work.

No matter what.

EPILOGUE

CHLOE

It was crazy how fast things changed.
Like milk going bad, or flowers dying, or panties getting
ripped in the "wash."
Dom could claim it was the machine, but I clearly heard a
rip.
And he still owed me ice cream.

ONE YEAR LATER

"Why would you put the sofa there? You can't see the TV properly."

I put my hands on my hips and stared at Dom. "Well, where should it go?"

He pointed with a handful of popcorn. "Under the window."

"We don't have blinds yet, and that's where the sun will come in. Have you considered that we might not be able to see anything?"

"Move the TV, then."

"We can't. That's the only spot it can go."

He sighed, shoving his handful of popcorn into his mouth. "I don't know what to tell you, Chlo."

"You can put the popcorn down and help me move this stuff, for a start." I waved a hand at the boxes that were piled on top of the coffee table.

"But what about the sofa?"

"We'll buy a new sofa!" I ran my fingers through my hair. "God, this is old anyway."

"I told you we should have brought my sofa."

"You're so lucky the kitchen knives are packed!" I growled at him.

He grinned. "Living together is going to be so fun."

"Hmm." I picked up a box and put it on the floor, then grabbed another. "Why is a bathroom box in here?"

"I don't know. Ask Elliott. He's the one who put the boxes there."

"Why? Because you keep eating?"

"I have to eat the popcorn before Peyton gets it."

I sighed. "We did this last week. You know she's craving popcorn, and if she gets here and there's none left, I'm letting you take the full blame for it. You can take those pregnancy hormones by yourself, buddy."

He stilled, hand in the bag. "You know what? After how she burst into tears when Jake ate a handful of hers, I think I'll save her this."

"Yeah. Good idea." I rolled my eyes. "Can you help me now?"

He gave me an overexaggerated sigh and lifted up the bathroom box. "Is this for our bathroom or the main one?"

"I don't know." I shrugged. "You'll have to look inside."

"Why didn't you mark it?"

"Because it's your handwriting on the box." I grinned. "This one's on you, Dom."

"Fuck it."

A tiny gasp came from the doorway. "Uncle Dom saided a bad word!"

His eyes widened, and he turned to Briony. "Sssh. You can't tell anyone that!"

"She doesn't need to. I heard it," Peyton said in a dry tone, coming up behind her and smoothing her hair. "Dom—"

"I didn't know she was there," he said quickly. "I didn't hear you come in."

"That's because you didn't close the front door." She shimmied past Briony. "Daddy has your tablet," she said to her.

She quickly ran off to where Elliott was presumably unloading a handful of boxes from the back of the truck.

"How are you feeling?" I asked Peyton.

"Great," she said with a giant, fake smile. "I threw up my breakfast and can't fit in my pants anymore. I'm supposed to be past the vomit stage!"

"I'll put this in the main bathroom for now," Dom said, lugging the box out of the room.

I rolled my eyes. "He's an ass. If it helps, I stopped him from eating all the popcorn for you."

She cast her glance toward the sofa where he'd left the bag. "Bet he only left a little."

Elliott came in with a box in hand, followed by Jake. "This is the last of the kitchen stuff."

"Ugh, thank you. Are the knives in there?" I asked.

"I can tell moving day is going well," Jake said dryly. "This is the showery-stuff for Mellie's bride party or whatever it is. Where do you want this?"

"Ummm." Shit. I'd forgotten I'd had all that in my spare room. "Can you put it in the garage for now? All the boxes are clearly marked, so..."

"All the boxes? How much stuff do you need for a party? Isn't the wedding enough?"

"Well, there are balloons, and plates, and centerpieces, and presents," I started.

"And games, and bachelorette things, and more gifts, and banners," Peyton continued.

"I heard presents." Mellie bounced into the room, almost pushing Jake out of the way. Her eyes immediately zoned in on the Sharpie-scribbled "Mellie's Bridal Shower" on the side of the box. "Oooh! Are my presents in there?"

"Quick, run!" Peyton yelled around a mouthful of popcorn.

Jake turned and ran through the hall, swerving in just enough time to avoid Briony. Who had no chance of seeing a tall, muscular man coming toward her because she was too engrossed in YouTube.

With the skill only a young child could have, she wandered over to the sofa and climbed up next to Peyton. She stuck her hand out, and Peyton tilted the bag so she could reach for it.

Just in time for Dom to walk in.

"Peyt. Seriously? Why will you share with her but not anyone else?" He held out his hands.

With a completely serious face, Peyton looked up and said, "I like her."

"Oh, well, that covers it," he muttered, moving the last box off the coffee table. "Where am I putting the table?"

"Outside," I said. "Where do you think it's going?"

"This is going to be a long day."

Elliott's laughter announced his return to the room. He smacked Dom on the shoulder, chuckled again, and headed outside.

"I think I regret this," Dom said.

"If you don't already," I replied, grabbing the end of the coffee table to pull it across the carpet. "You will when I unpack the knives."

***

I closed the door to the dishwasher and leaned against the counter. The laughter coming from my living room made me happy. The boxes everywhere? Not so much.

But they would disappear in time. I knew that. Especially if I took control of the unpacking, because God only knew nothing would ever get done if Dom was in charge.

A hard, familiar body pressed against my back, and Dom's strong arms wrapped around my shoulders as he kissed the side of my neck. "Okay?"

I nodded. "It's weird, isn't it? Knowing this house is ours."

"Yep. And we have so much space. This is definitely better than staying at my old apartment."

"Which I hated," I added, touching his arm. "Isn't it weird how everything changed?"

"For who?"

"All of us. Did you think we'd be here eighteen months ago?"

He shook his head. "Honestly? I never thought you and I would ever break through the barrier that we had between us, never mind any of this. Especially Peyton being pregnant."

"No kidding. That's the weirdest one of all. I would have sworn on my grave that she would never have gotten pregnant. Ever."

"You're not the only person. I guess filing the adoption papers changed her mind completely about parenthood."

"Well, she couldn't have Elliott without Bri," I said. "She told me they're due in court in two weeks to finalize the adoption. Bri wouldn't stop talking about it. She's so excited for Peyton to be her mom."

"Poor kid," he muttered. "She has no idea what she's getting into."

I laughed and tapped his arm. "She's a great mom to her, and you know it."

"I do. But I'm still her brother, so…"

"Dom."

He chuckled. "Do you think we'll have kids?"

"Yeah, but we're doing gender selection, because nobody needs another Dom running around this planet. One is more than enough."

"A girl could turn out like Peyton. We share genes, remember?"

"Crap. I guess it's a potluck, huh?"

"Something like that, yeah." He kissed the side of my head again. "I'm glad we did this."

"So am I." I leaned into him, briefly closing my eyes.

He held me a little tighter, and I relaxed into his hold. It was perfect—it always had been. And, against the odds, we'd made it this long.

A part of me still wondered if we could actually do it. The fear that one day I would lose him completely was something I didn't think I would ever get rid of, but I was so glad I made the choice not to let it rule me.

The only thing I regretted was that we'd taken so long to admit to each other how we felt. And, you know what? I'd never been so glad to go on a date with another guy or see him go out with another woman.

Without that, I knew exactly where we'd be. We'd be in the same office, having the same fights. I'd be saving him the last piece of pizza, and he'd be doing all the little things around the office, so I never had to.

It still amazed me that he could do all that, but he was basically unable to pay the internet company until I took control over that.

Then again, he was a little strange like that. Can't keep a key in his pocket to save his life, but printer ink?

Sign. Him. Up.

"Chlo?" Dom whispered in my ear.

"Yeah?"

"I saved you the last piece of pizza."

And that, right there, was true love.

THE END

COMING SOON FROM EMMA HART...

FOUR DAY FLING

...a romantic comedy of epically awkward proportions.

Imagine this.
You're ready to leave after a one-night stand, and you're figuring out how to—shock horror—leave your number and ask him to be your fake boyfriend for your sister's wedding this weekend.
When he wakes up.

Well, that happened to me. And over coffee and omelets, I found myself a date.
Which was how I ended up arriving at the wedding with a guy I knew nothing about.
I didn't know his last name, or how we met, or how long we'd been dating. I didn't know where he grew up, what he'd majored in in college, or how many siblings he had.
I sure as hell didn't know he was Adam Winters, hotshot hockey player, and not only my father's favorite player, but my little nephew's freakin' idol.
Which means I'm in trouble. Big, big trouble.

My mother is suspicious, my sister is bridezilla on crack, and my grandpa will tell anyone who'll listen about his time in Amsterdam's Red Light District.

Four days.

I have to keep this up for four days, and then Adam and I can return to our regular lives, where we don't have sex whenever we're alone, and my family aren't interrogating him over his intentions with me.

At least, that's the plan.
And we all know what happens to those...

Releasing July 24th!

Visit www.emmahart.org/four-day-fling for all pre-order links!

BOOKS BY EMMA HART

Standalones:
Blind Date
Being Brooke
Catching Carly
Casanova
Mixed Up
Miss Fix-It
Miss Mechanic
The Upside to Being Single
The Hook-Up Experiment
The Dating Experiment
Four Day Fling (coming July 24th)
Hot Mess (coming September 25th)
Tequila, Tequila (coming November 13th)

The Vegas Nights series:
Sin
Lust

Stripped series:
Stripped Bare
Stripped Down

The Burke Brothers:
Dirty Secret
Dirty Past
Dirty Lies
Dirty Tricks

Dirty Little Rendezvous

The Holly Woods Files:
Twisted Bond
Tangled Bond
Tethered Bond
Tied Bond
Twirled Bond
Burning Bond
Twined Bond

By His Game series:
Blindsided
Sidelined
Intercepted

Call series:
Late Call
Final Call
His Call

Wild series:
Wild Attraction
Wild Temptation
Wild Addiction
Wild: The Complete Series

The Game series:
The Love Game
Playing for Keeps
The Right Moves
Worth the Risk

Memories series:
Never Forget
Always Remember

ABOUT THE AUTHOR

Emma Hart is the New York Times and USA TODAY bestselling author of over thirty novels and has been translated into several different languages.

She is a mother, wife, lover of wine, Pink Goddess, and valiant rescuer of wild baby hedgehogs.

Emma prides herself on her realistic, snarky smut, with comebacks that would make a PMS-ing teenage girl proud.

Yes, really. She's that sarcastic.

You can find her online at:
www.emmahart.org
www.facebook.com/emmahartbooks
www.instagram.com/EmmaHartAuthor
www.pinterest.com/authoremmahart

Alternatively, you can join her reader group at http://bit.ly/EmmaHartsHartbreakers.

You can also get all things Emma to your email inbox by signing up for Emma Alerts*.
http://bit.ly/EmmaAlerts

*Emails sent for sales, new releases, pre-order availability, and cover reveals. Each cover reveal contains an exclusive excerpt.

18406996R00139

Made in the USA
Middletown, DE
30 November 2018